Lucy brings her grandmother Martha, in hospital
recovering from an operation, a bunch of lilac.

Suddenly the past is unlocked, as Martha
remembers the seven days in May when she entered the
world of 1798, meeting some of the leading figures of the
day – Viceroy Camden, Lord Clare, Lord Castlereagh,
John Philpot Curran, Jonah Barrington, the informer
Leonard McNally.

The shadow of Lord Edward Fitzgerald is ever present
and the dramatic story of his near escapes and final
capture is interwoven with the day to day life of a great
house in Merrion Square and the Merrion family –
to Lady Abigail and Clarissa, her daughter,
Martha is the 'cousin' from Donegal.

The rising tide of rebellion touches all their lives,
particularly those of Matilda, Lady Abigail's companion,
and James, the tutor, both of whom are caught up in the
revolutionary movement of the United Irishmen . . .

D0238542

Yvonne MacGrory

Martha and the Ruby Ring

Pauline   Fallon

Illustrated by Terry Myler

Pauline   Fallon
Age   12
6th   Class -

THE CHILDREN'S PRESS

For my sisters and brothers –
Cathal, Deirdre, Patricia, Enda, Hugh,
Alex, Bernadette, Stella, Angela, Caroline, Irene,
and in memory of Leonard and Margaret

First published 1993 by
The Children's Press
45 Palmerston Road, Dublin 6

© Text Yvonne MacGrory 1993
© Illustrations The Children's Press 1993

ISBN 0 947962 77 8

Typesetting by Computertype Limited
Printed by Colour Books Limited

Contents

1 Lilacs

'Don't forget the flowers,' Paul McLaughlin gave Lucy a quick pat on the head as he went by on his way out of the kitchen.

'Dad, do you think I'm feather-brained or what?' Lucy pushed an unruly reddish-brown curl back from her forehead.

'Bird-brained, more likely,' murmured her brother David.

'You watch it,' warned Lucy, 'and get a move on or we'll be late for school . . . of course I'll remember the flowers.'

'Just a reminder!' Paul and his wife Jean exchanged smiles. 'In case your marvellous memory goes on the blink. We have some very nice bouquets at the moment. All done up with cellophane. Ribbons thrown in for free.'

Paul McLaughlin was the manager of the local supermarket.

'Get nice cheerful colours,' said Jean. 'Pale and pretty. Last time I was in a nursing home someone sent me a bunch of rust-coloured chrysanthemums. They were so depressing. Couldn't wait to get rid of them.'

'This is turning out to be Operation Supergran,' groaned Lucy, as she got up and rushed out to the hall to collect her school things. She put her head back around the door. 'Mum! After school I'll go and see Gran – with the flowers – and then I'm going swimming with Noreen. So I won't be home until about six.'

'I don't like to see you going that long without food,' said her mother. 'Are you sure you have enough lunch with you? Get yourself a bar of chocolate.'

'They'll give me a cup of tea and a biscuit at the nursing home,' said Lucy. 'Do stop worrying. You'd think I was next door to anorexia.'

'Don't stay too long. Remember she's still convalescing.'

'I'll time it,' Lucy displayed her new swatch watch, 'anyway, I'm meeting Noreen at five, so I can't overstay . . . Do hurry, David. Have you got your sports gear?'

Then they were gone – Paul, Lucy and David – and Jean sat down for another, and more relaxed, cup of tea.

Gran, Paul's mother, was recovering from an operation. It had been a severe operation but she had come through it successfully. Now all she needed was rest. Jean had wanted her to come straight to them after the hospital but then she and Paul decided that a convalescent home for a fortnight would give her far more peace than was possible in a house with two healthy children who lived at a fairly high rate of decibels.

Jean usually visited her in the afternoon but today she had an ICA meeting and Lucy had volunteered. Gran would be delighted to see her; they had had a special relationship ever since Gran had given Lucy the beautiful ruby ring.

The nursing home was at the top of one of those steep hills which are characteristic of so many Donegal towns and villages. As Lucy pushed her bicycle up the long slope she thought about the ruby ring. Gran had given it to her on her eleventh birthday, and when she was examining the box in which it had come she found written on the inside in gold lettering an extraordinary message telling her of the ring's magic powers. Lucy had made a wish and found herself back in the Ireland of 1885. She remembered so vividly every part of that strange experience, especially her friendship with Elizabeth and Robert at Langley Castle and the story of Nellie the scullery-maid.

She had often wondered if Gran, who had been given the ring by *her* grandmother, had found the message in the box and used the ring to make a wish. From the twinkle in her eyes once or twice when it was mentioned, Lucy was sure that she had. But somehow there never seemed to have been an opportunity to ask her about it. Maybe today? But, no! Lucy remembered her mother's warning: 'She's still weak after the op. Only cheerful conversation. No bad news. No arguments. No deaths.' (Lucy couldn't refrain from asking mischievously, 'Why, who's died lately that I didn't hear about?')

No, her mother was right. Nothing serious. Talk about school. Swimming. Practising for the school sports. Tell her about David making the junior soccer team. Getting top of the class today in general knowledge. *That* should please her.

Lucy paused. She was nearly at the top of the long hill. Hooray! No doubt about it; the view was spectacular. The glittering expanse of Donegal Bay far below, the great mass of Crownard to the west, the distant Blue Stacks on the northern horizon. Anyone would get well in a place like this!

As she set off again, she thought of what she would say when she went in: 'Hi, Gran!' Voice bright and cheerful. 'Great to see you looking so well. Here are some . . .'

She stopped and groaned aloud. She had forgotten the flowers!

How *could* she have been such an idiot. Dad and Mum were right. She was a feather-brain. Worse, a bird-brain. She had thought about the flowers all day long. But in the excitement of coming first and then arranging with Noreen about swimming she had just dashed away from school on her bicycle and clean forgotten about going to the super-market. Now what was she to do? She couldn't go back all that way, walk up the hill again, see Gran and be in time for swimming. And she didn't want to visit Gran without bringing her something.

A sudden thought struck her. A little way back was Shovlins' farmhouse. As she had passed it, the scent of lilac came to her so strongly that she had stopped to admire the huge bush growing at the entrance. She'd go back and ask Mrs Shovlin for a few flowers. Surely she wouldn't mind. Not for Gran, convalescing from a serious operation.

Lucy was in luck. Mrs Shovlin was at home, in the kitchen making bread. She wiped her hands on her apron and followed Lucy out to the lilac-bush.

'It's for Gran. I meant to bring her flowers and I forgot. Just a branch or two. They are so beautiful and the scent is fantastic, isn't it? There are so many you'll never miss one or two. Anyway, Mum says it's summer pruning and encourages more flowers. Oh, please, Mrs Shovlin.'

Mrs Shovlin couldn't help smiling at the impassioned outpouring. 'Of course. We'll get the secateurs or a knife. Wait a moment.'

When she came back, her face had a worried look. 'I'm just remembering something,' she told Lucy as she cut a few stems. 'About your Gran and lilac. There was something about a bush being cut down. Or maybe I'm mixing her up with someone else. It was all so long ago.'

'I'm sure you are,' said Lucy firmly, adding hastily, 'It couldn't have been anything to do with Gran. She loves flowers . . . Oh, Mrs Shovlin, you've saved my life. I'll never be able to thank you enough.'

Gran was sitting up in bed, looking pretty in a pale pink bedjacket. Still very frail, thought Lucy, as she went over to the bed and laid the lilac beside her. The overpowering fragrance of the flowers filled the room, seeming to bring it the essence of summer, of long days, luminous twilights, and flowers innumerable scattered through the long grasses by the wayside.

'Sorry they're not gift-wrapped,' said Lucy. 'But aren't they glorious? I'll get the nurse to put them in water at once. And every time you look at them you'll know that summer is really here again and soon you'll be out in the sunshine . . .'

She broke off. Her grandmother had buried her face in the lilac blossoms. When she looked up again, Lucy could see that she was crying. Uncontrollable sobs shook her thin shoulders.

A nurse rushed in. 'What's happening? What did you do to upset your grandmother? Mrs McLaughlin, you mustn't worry about a thing. I'll get you a nice cup of tea.' She glared at Lucy, who was standing by, bewildered. 'Then

you can lie down. Peace and quiet. That's what you need. And no visitors.'

Lucy thought she was about to be banished. For what? What had she done that had brought on such an unexpected reaction?

Then suddenly Gran smiled. 'It's all right, Nurse. It had nothing to do with Lucy. I want her to stay. But I would be glad of the tea – bring a cup for her as well.'

'Will I put the flowers in water?'

'No, leave them for the moment. I'll get Lucy to do it.'

When the nurse went away, Lucy turned an anguished face to Gran.

'It *was* something I did. What was it? Was it the lilac?' She remembered Mrs Shovlin's hesitation. Now it was as clear as daylight. Gran hated lilac – Lucy had brought back some unpleasant memory. How could she have been so stupid. If only she'd gone to the supermarket Gran would now be admiring harmless carnations and gypsophila and chatting happily, instead of being in tears, with that lost look on her face.

Lucy went to the window, uncertain as to what to do next. 'I'll never live this down,' she thought to herself. 'That nurse will tell Mum and Dad when they come up tonight. And serve me right.' But worst of all was the thought that she had upset Gran.

'Lucy.' She turned at the soft voice. Gran had wiped away her tears and was now smiling. 'Oh, Lucy, forgive me. I just couldn't help myself. The lilacs brought it all back ...'

'Brought what back, Gran?'

'Lucy, the ruby ring. Did you ever wonder whether I had used it?'

'I did, of course. I always meant to ask you. but somehow there never seemed to be the right opportunity.'

'Well, I did . . . and I'm going to tell you all about it. Not today. But come back tomorrow and I'll start the story . . .

it'll probably take several afternoons. That is if you have the time.'

'Oh, but I do. I want to hear the story. I've always been dying with curiosity, wanting to ask you, then afraid to mention it . . . Anyway, Mum says you'll be coming home this weekend. Then we'll have all the time in the world . . . just tell me now, why did you cry when you saw the lilacs?

'Because of Andrew. When I first met him it was May and the lilacs were in bloom . . .'

'Your tea.' The nurse was back. She grudgingly gave Lucy a biscuit, as if she still blamed her for upsetting her patient.

'Now, off you go,' said Gran when Lucy had finished. 'Enjoy your swimming. And come back tomorrow.'

The nurse saw Lucy out. 'I don't know what all that was about. But your Gran seems in really good form now. You had some effect on her!'

'How was Gran?' asked her mother when Lucy finally got home.

'Great. Looking forward to coming home in the weekend.'

'Did you remember the flowers?' asked her father who had just come in. 'I didn't see you in the shop.'

'Yes, I gave her flowers. And she loved them,' said Lucy slowly.

After supper she went straight up to her room. 'Hardly spoke a word since she came home . . . I hope she's not sickening for something.' Her mother's worried voice followed her up the stairs, followed by soothing reassurances from her father.

Lucy took out the ruby ring from her top drawer and looked at it for a long time, turning it this way and that so that the red lights in its depths glittered and glowed.

What would Gran's story be?

2 Martha Makes a Wish

'Actually,' said Gran. 'I didn't discover the secret of the ruby ring until I was sixteen.'

She was sitting propped up by pillows, wearing pale blue today, looking more cheerful and relaxed than on the previous day.

'But I thought you were given the ring when you were eleven. Like me.' Lucy was puzzled.

'Oh, I got the ring all right. But I had such small hands that it kept slipping off my finger. So my parents decided it must be put away until I was older. I didn't argue. One didn't in those days – parents knew best. I was allowed to fit it on every birthday until at last, on my sixteenth birthday, the ring, although still a little loose, stayed on my finger. I was so pleased. You see, I was going to my first dance, what we used to call a "hop" in those days.'

She smiled. 'I was considered rather a good-looking girl in my day – not that anyone in the family would have told me, in case I got a swelled head.'

'Dad showed me a photograph of you only the other day. You had long dark hair with floppy waves over one eye . . . totally non-cool your hairstyle . . . but you really were very pretty! Dad said that photo was taken on your sixteenth birthday.'

'All rather a long time ago now!'

'And the dance, I mean the hop? Did you enjoy it?'

'No, Lucy . . . I didn't enjoy it at all.'

'Oh, Gran. Your first dance and your birthday and all. What happened?'

'Well, it was May 1944. Have you any idea of what was happening then, Lucy?'

'Of course. Second World War.'

'It was talked about a lot, especially by the men, old and young. Ireland was neutral, but my father had a cousin in the Commandos, so he and my brothers took a particular interest in the war news. Everybody knew somebody who was in the war.

'We weren't badly off in Ireland. Not compared to the dreadful things that were happening everywhere else – though we didn't know the half of it then. But there was rationing here. Things like tea, sugar and butter. And you couldn't buy any clothes without coupons.

'I just turned sixteen. I wanted to enjoy myself. I wanted to wear beautiful clothes, silk stockings, dance with handsome strangers to the music of a big orchestra like the ones they had in Hollywood movies. In short – and I know this may seem very silly and frivolous to you – I wanted excitement and glamour and romance.'

'Oh, poor Gran,' said Lucy sympathetically. 'That doesn't seem at all silly to me.' She thought with a blush about the 'big house' that led to *her* ruby ring adventure. 'We all want something we haven't got.'

'Well!' A rueful smile. 'All I got was a hop in the local school hall. Me in my full-skirted cotton dress and sensible sandals. The local boys in their grey flannels and bicycle clips, Brylcreemed hair and sweaty palms. I knew them all – not a *thrawneen* of glamour among the lot of them. The music was two old men playing the fiddle and the piano accordian. Dullsville, as we used to say.

'I knew I was being very unfair. Why did I expect the boys to turn into Robert Taylors and the girls to look like Hedy Lamarr, and the school hall to have a shining floor? I

should have seen how genuine and friendly it all was
. . . but I didn't. I just knew it wasn't my idea of a first
dance.

'Later, when you read *Madame Bovary* you'll know how I
felt. I couldn't tell my family or my friends – they wouldn't
have understood – but there was something in me that was
crying out for new experiences, new people . . .

'Yes, I remember the night of my sixteenth birthday so
well . . .

'When the hop was over, at twelve midnight sharp, a
crowd of us walked home together. I was to stay with a
cousin that night but I suddenly decided I wanted to be
alone. There was a glorious full moon, the hawthorn trees
were like ghosts in the hedges, and I could feel spring surg-
ing all around me. It seemed such a waste of a beautiful
night to go into someone's dark kitchen, drink cocoa, and
talk about who got off with who. So I told my cousin I had
to go home.

'The house was in darkness, everyone was in bed. I crept
upstairs, and for a while I knelt at the window looking at the
moonlight filtering through the cypress grove. The box with
the ruby ring was open on the window-sill in front of me.
Everyone had admired it at the dance. No one had ever
seen a ruby before, let alone a star ruby. I told them all
about my grandmother, about granduncle James and how
he saved the life of an Indian Rajah and was rewarded with
the gift of a ruby ring, which he was told had magical powers. I'm sure they didn't believe a word of it.

'But I felt it was something special. I loved the ring. I
even loved the box. I was stroking the soft lining inside the
lid when there was a click and the lid just split apart. I was
upset. I thought I had broken it. Then I noticed some writing in small gold letters, and I held the box up to the moonlight to get a better look. The words I read sent my heart
racing:

The secret of this Ruby Ring,
Is that two wishes it can bring.
On right hand, middle finger, place,
Then turn the ring around but twice,
Now, make your wish, then wait and see,
How magic, the Ruby Ring can be

'I was dumbfounded. I didn't know what to think.'

'Gran, I felt the very same. Isn't it strange? I'd almost forgotten what the words were until you reminded me.'

'Actually, I forgot them myself for many years. Somehow today I can remember everything so clearly.

'Well, I read the wording again and I thought of all the things I would like to have. A new bicycle? I'll wish for a new bicycle. We cycled everywhere in those days. My mother and I shared an ancient curved monstrosity. Black, naturally. Nothing then like your bright pink or green mountain bikes.' Gran smiled.

'But then I thought of my mother, your great-grandmother. How could I explain away a new bicycle? She would have thought it was stolen and brought it to the garda barracks. I'd have to think of something else.

'My mother had a very rigid view of life. "Waste not, want not." "What can't be cured must be endured." That kind of thing. I suppose she must have loved my father at some stage but she never showed any signs of affection. Her main interest in life was work. All day. Every day. There wasn't a frivolous bone in her body. I think it stemmed from her Scottish ancestry – her mother was from there. In later years I came to appreciate her good qualities – she had rock-like strength in the face of a crisis. But when I was sixteen we didn't understand each other at all.

'I only remember one occasion when I actually saw her laughing. Some cousins came on a visit and mother worked miracles and produced a lovely tea – things were very formal in those days, with a tray, a tray-cloth, a silver-plated teapot and sandwiches and cakes. They were particularly struck with the "banana" sandwiches. Because there just weren't any bananas in those years. My mother explained they were made from parsnips mashed with a little sugar. The elder cousin, who knew what a banana tasted like, said she wouldn't have known the difference. How Mother glowed at the praise . . .

'There was another reason why I was feeling a little rebellious that evening. For the past few years I'd been going for piano lessons to a Frau Hassler – she taught music in the Convent of Mercy in Strabane and retired to live here.'

Lucy's eyes had wandered to the window. 'What's all this got to do with the ruby ring?' she wondered, impatient for Gran to get to the point.

'I know you want to hurry me along,' said Gran with a smile, 'but this is of real relevance to my story. Frau Hassler had a lot to do with my wish and she comes into the story later. So listen . . .

'I went to her once a week for an hour. Half the time was for the piano. Then she used to talk to me. About Austria, the Hapsburgs, the Hofberg, Schönbrunn, Emperor Franz Josef, the court balls, the clothes, the dances. Not from first-hand experience of course, but from stories, newspaper reports and so on. Mother thought it was all a waste of time and wanted me to give up going to Frau Hassler's . . . She didn't see that it was the only breath of the outside world that I had and, with the war on, was likely to have for the next few years . . .

'No, I knew Mother wouldn't have understood about the ruby ring, or making a wish, or wanting a more exciting life. I remember thinking, "I'll have to wish for something that I won't have to explain to Mother."

'And then it came to me. Something that had been sim-

mering in my mind all evening. I was tired of the life I was
living. I was the only girl among eight brothers – imagine
eight brothers! All with shirts to be washed and ironed. No
drip dry then. I didn't mind helping – I wouldn't have felt it
fair to leave all the work to Mother. But there was just so
much of it. When I came in from school, I did my home-
work. Then there were meals to be prepared, washing-up to
be done, hens to be fed, floors to be washed, kitchen tables
to be scrubbed, and the endless laundry. The boys all had
their jobs, with the cattle, the farm, the hay and the turf.
But they could sit around the fire at night while Mother and
I were turning sheets and mending socks. I seemed to be
working endlessly. She could have had a maid – there were
plenty in those days – but she was so particular she
wouldn't – said they were all useless.

'I suddenly decided that the one thing I wanted in life
was to be spoiled and pampered, to be the centre of atten-

tion, to feel beautiful and loved. Mind, I didn't ask for all this in one wish! I made a humble enough request. I thought that if I could go to one magnificent ball, just for one night, I would be happy ever after.

'As I was to stay at my cousin's for a day, I felt my absence wouldn't be noticed – I wasn't too worried about that aspect of things. I figured that was up to the ruby ring to sort out. I only half believed in it anyway.'

'And is that what happened, Gran?' Lucy's eyes were shining, all impatience gone. 'Did you get to your great ball and be home before anyone knew you had gone . . . at least you didn't have a Cinderella deadline!'

'Well, as you must know, things don't work out exactly as we plan them . . . I sat on the window-sill, put the ring on my right middle finger, twisted it twice, and said, "I want to go to a truly magnificent ball."

'I closed my eyes, then sat up in a panic. I hadn't mentioned a dress! And I wanted the most wonderful dress in the world. And now my wish was made and I felt I'd made a mess of it.

'I lay back and closed my eyes again. I remember feeling a little foolish. Just because I wanted something so badly I was willing to believe the ruby ring could give it to me. Maybe it was all nonsense.

'I tried to open my eyes but they just wouldn't open. Then I began to feel peculiar, rather faint and dizzy . . .

'A loud thud brought me to my senses. My first thought was that I had fallen and that Mother and Father would be in to see what had happened. But then I realized that the noise I had heard was not the sound of someone falling. It was the banging of a door, a carriage door. I could open my eyes again. I was standing on the pavement of a city street, with tall houses stretching away on either side. Houses of glowing rose-coloured brick, fluted pillars framing the doors, shining brass knockers, and semi-circle fanlights of leaded glass.

'Some people passed by, the women in long high-waisted dresses and short jackets, the men in cut-away coats, tight breeches, shining knee-high boots and tall hats. "There must be a fancy-dress dance somewhere," I thought. "So that's where I'm going! Well, at least it's better than the school hall."

'I suddenly realised that I, too, was wearing a long, high-waisted dress, so I decided it must be one of those dances where everyone is asked to come in the costume of the same period. But what were we all doing walking around the streets? Where was the ballroom? And my dress wasn't really a ball-gown. I felt cheated.

'There was a discreet cough behind me and I turned around. The door I had heard banging belonged to a carriage that was still standing there, and someone dressed in livery was unloading two trunks from the back. The coachman was smiling at me. He gestured to the three steps leading up to the door, then went ahead and knocked. I followed him and we both stood there for a few moments. The door opened. An imposing-looking man inclined his head at me. "Ah, Miss Martha. Did you have a good journey? Thanks, Joseph. Bring in the trunks. Mulligan, take the horses around . . . This way, Miss."

'I followed him into a wide hallway, the walls of which were splendidly decorated with plasterwork of delicate frothing leaves and flowers which enclosed medallions of female heads and framed two big oil paintings, one a view of a country house and landscape, the other of horses and hounds in a hunt setting. An ornate bronze and glass lantern hung from the high ceiling. The floor was of white marble with small black lozenges set in at intervals. A massive mahogany door led into an inner hall, from where a staircase with mahogany banisters led upstairs.

'At the top of a flight of stairs was another landing and another mahogany door. The butler (I presumed he was either a butler or a footman) opened it. He paused, cleared his throat, bowed and said, "Miss Martha, your Ladyship."

'As I went in my mind was a jumble of feelings. The ruby ring was magic all right. I had been transported to another century – which one I wasn't quite sure yet. But strangely I wasn't too worried. I knew I could get back home. I patted the ring (which I now wore on my left hand, just in case I might make an inadvertent wish). It was my passport to home. Thus reassured, I decided to enjoy myself. After all, there was the ball to come!

'There were three women in the morning-room (as I later learned it was called). Or rather, one woman and two

girls. The woman whom the butler had addressed as 'Your
Ladyship' extended a languid hand and I went over to her
as she lay reclining on a long sofa. She was magnificently
dressed in amythest-coloured satin, cut away in the front to
show a paler-coloured brocaded underskirt. The sleeves fell
to just below her elbows and underneath were cream under-
sleeves, bound with pearl ropes. Pearls also decorated the
tight bodice.

' "Martha! Do let me take a look at you. It's so many
years since we last met. Your poor father has no sense keep-
ing you in the wilds of Donegal . . . where does he expect
you to meet anyone? Yes . . ." her inspection seemed to be
complete. ". . . you have the Cobbett looks all right. We are
a handsome family," she gestured to the young girl standing
behind her.

'I looked enviously at her simple high-waisted dress of
some floating fabric in very pale pink. I suddenly felt the
country cousin in my dark travelling dress and cloak.

' "I'm so glad you arrived in time for Clarissa's birthday.
What an extraordinary coincidence! That my sister and I
had daughters on two succeeding days. Your birthday was
yesterday, was it not? Clarissa's is today. We're having a
party for her tonight. Nothing very lavish. Dinner for about
twenty. Have you anything to wear?" She looked rather critically at my dress. "Matilda, go upstairs and see if there is
anything more suitable for Martha to wear tonight."

'I must have blushed (what on earth was in the trunk I
wondered) because Lady Abigail looked at me and laughed.
"Don't let it concern you. It's just that what is considered
fashionable in Donegal may not be at all suitable for
Dublin. We'll probably have to get you a complete
trousseau. I did promise your poor mother that you should
have a season to remember, or at least what's left of it now.
It's too bad you missed so much . . . the season really closes
on St Patrick's Day. Still there will be plenty of entertain-

ment between dinners and the theatre and suppers, and you are luckily in time for the ball at the Viceregal Lodge. That will be, let me see, tomorrow. The eighteenth. Let's hope nothing happens to upset that . . ."

' "What do you mean?" I asked.

' "My dear, you're so insulated in the country. We've had such a time here. Nothing but alarms and excursions."

' "Mama is talking about the political unrest," said Clarissa. She was a very pretty girl, with pale golden hair, but I suspected that she could hardly get a word in edgeways with her voluble mother.

' "Merrion is pessimistic – as usual – but I was talking to Lord Camden last night and he assured me that things are on the mend. I suppose we must be grateful to General Lake. Though I do not support some of his methods."

'I was thinking hard, I need hardly tell you. Camden? General Lake? They didn't mean a thing to me. Really, how inadequate is history teaching. We learn about events. The people who make them are usually forgotten.

'By this time Matilda had come back, evidently with a negative report on "my" wardrobe. She shook her head at Lady Abigail, who sighed as she looked at me.

' "Well, she can't wear *that*. The sleeves are set so badly. Clarissa, you're much the same size. Give Martha your lavender-sprigged muslin with the mauve ribbons. It will look quite well on her, suit her colouring."

' "Mama, everyone has seen that dress a dozen times. They'll know it's mine."

' "We'll say there was a mix-up over the trunks. That they were left behind at the last stage . . . Now, Martha, you'd better go and get ready. Dinner will be at four . . . Matilda, you take Martha to her room . . ."

'As I followed Matilda up the curving staircase my head was in a spin. I was going to a great ball. But it wasn't to be held until tomorrow. I could only hope I would get home

before my absence was noticed. Then I calmed down. I'd trust in the power of the ruby ring. I relaxed and admired the decoration on the walls, which had the same beautiful sculptures of garlands of flowers and leaves that I had seen in the hall.

'On the second floor, Matilda paused before a door. "This is the schoolroom," she said.

'I was about to ask who would be there when I suddenly remembered that I would be supposed to know all about the family. So I just smiled.

' "We'll go in,' said Matilda, pushing open the door. A thin young man in dark clothes and two boys of about ten years of age were sitting at an old scarred table. The man jumped to his feet, his face alight with pleasure.

' "Why, Miss Matilda, what a surprise!"

'Matilda's colour had deepened to a becoming flush as she looked at him. He, in turn, had eyes only for her.

' "I have brought Miss Martha, Lady Abigail's god-daughter and Clarissa's cousin, to meet the twins," said Matilda, adding to me, "This is James the tutor, and of course you will remember Cecil and Cedric."

'The two blond-haired blue-eyed boys, very like Clarissa I thought, stared at me solemnly.

' "Boys," said James reprovingly, "have you no greeting for your cousin?"

' "Greetings, Cousin Martha," they said dutifully.

' "What are you teaching them?" I asked.

' "His Lordship and Her Ladyship have given me specific instructions. French, writing and arithmetic are to be particularly attended to. Later they will study music, dancing, fencing and drawing. And they are to be perfect masters of history, particularly of their own country."

'I picked up a book from the table and read the title: *The Rights of Man* by Thomas Paine. "Surely that's a little advanced for them?"

'He laughed. "I'm afraid that's my own private reading, Miss Martha. While they are writing, I read."

'I had vaguely heard of *The Rights of Man*, which I seemed to equate with liberty, equality and fraternity. It didn't quite seem to fit in with Lady Abigail and the opulence of the house in which I now found myself.

' "You can buy these books here?" I couldn't help asking.

' "We have an excellent bookseller in Grafton Street, Patrick Byrne. He keeps us informed of all the latest . . ."

'Matilda was frowning at him and he broke off, saying, "Well, Cecil, have you finished? Let me see . . ."

' "We'd better hurry," said Matilda, "if you are to be ready in time." The colour had left her cheeks and she seemed a little flustered. I couldn't help wondering if there was romance in the air and why *The Rights of Man* had upset her. However, she had recovered herself by the time we went up another flight of stairs. Throwing open a door, she said, "Lady Abigail thought you might like it here. She felt it would remind you of the country, as it looks over the square." She laughed and added, "Lady Abigail hates the country. Even going to Carton and Castletown. Says it's a penance and can't wait to get back to Dublin."

' "How lovely," I said as I looked at the four-poster bed, its deep pink curtains tied back to reveal a white bedspread sprigged with tiny rosebuds.

'A red-cheeked girl dropped a curtsey. "This is Breege," said Matilda. "She'll look after you. Now I'd better go down and supervise preparations. All that china and glass and silver to be checked over!"

' "Let me take your hat," said Breege. She already had the lilac-sprigged muslin spread out on the bed. I handed her my small black straw hat. "And your spencer, Miss."

' "My what? . . . oh yes," I suddenly realised that she was indicating my short jacket.

'She poured water from a small rose-patterned jug into a delft basin and I washed my face and arms. Then she indicated the dressing-table. I sat down. Someone to do my hair. What utter luxury! Breege brushed back my dark curls, parted my hair, brushed it again, combed and twisted and twirled it. "You have lovely thick hair, Miss Martha. No need for a piece at all."

' "A piece?"

' "Yes, most ladies need them to fluff out their hair. But yours is so springy and curly, and it falls so naturally."

She deftly inserted a fancy hair-comb and showed me her handiwork. My reflection smiled back. My unruly curls had been tamed into little ringlets and curling strands which framed my face. It was perfect!

' "Now the dress . . . it is pretty, isn't it?" And so it was. It was light and airy, swirling around me as I moved. Then Breege produced a pair of stockings with mauve 'clocks' just above the ankles. "What's the point of them," I laughed. "Nobody will see them."

' "Well," Breege smiled wisely. "They sometimes show. And they're the *ton*."

'A pair of satin slippers and I was ready. Martha, the kitchen drudge, was going to a party. Not to the bare walls and drab colouring of the school hall but to an elegant gathering in a beautiful house, where everyone would be splendidly dressed. There would be food and wine, laughter and sparking conversation.

' "Now, you're ready for the drawing-room." Breege looked me over critically and seemed satisfied with her efforts. "I'll show you down. It's on the first floor."

'As we went down the stairs together, my confidence was swelling like a bubble inside me, growing stronger by the minute, until I was almost floating on air. Pausing by the huge gilt-framed looking-glass on the landing to the right of the drawing-room door, I looked at myself.

'Was this really me? This ethereal girl with the lovely dark curls, slim as a wand, in a floating dress that palely glimmered in the misty depths of the glass . . .'

'Gran,' said Lucy when her grandmother stopped, 'you were much smarter than I was. You got high life. All I got was kitchen work!'

Her grandmother's eyes twinkled. 'Well, I came from the kitchen – and went up in the world. You were living in very comfortable circumstances – and you went down. Maybe there's a moral there.'

'Did you know what year you had gone back to?'

'Not exactly. I knew I was in Dublin in one of the Georgian squares. There was unrest and two well-known people of the time were Camden and General Lake . . .'

The nurse came in. 'Time up. Off you go . . . You're taking Mrs McLaughlin home tomorrow, aren't you?'

'I'll finish the story then,' promised Gran.

Martha's
Story

3   *Clarissa's Birthday*

Martha paused on the landing outside the drawing-room door. It was slightly ajar but she was almost afraid to push it open. Looking well was one thing, but how would she carry off a party for twenty people, at which there were sure to be relations who could immediately spot that she was an imposter. She might say something which would betray that she was from another age. Or someone might ask her a question she couldn't answer – more than likely as she didn't even know what year it was! What would she do then? She nervously fingered the ruby ring.

There was a light footstep on the stairs and Clarissa was beside her.

'How pretty you look!' she said, putting her arm around Martha's waist. 'That dress looks far better on you than it ever did on me. How do you like mine?' She twirled around, and the silver ribbons embroidered through her white dress glittered like falling stars.

'It's beautiful.'

'Mama had the fabric sent specially from London, but don't tell.'

'Why not?'

'We're supposed to wear home-manufactured cloths but they don't make this kind yet. Poor Mama – she hates the new fashions.'

'Why?'

'Because now everyone can look in fashion. All you need

31

is a length of white muslin, and *voilá,* you're *bon ton.* She preferred the days when it was all heavily embroidered satin and silk that the "lower orders",' Clarissa's voice adopted a mincing tone, 'couldn't copy. We tease her by telling her that since the French Revolution we're all equal now . . . Anyway, I love the new dresses. I wasn't looking forward to growing-up and having to wear stays and hoops and heavy fabrics. Now fashions are divine . . . come, let's go in.' Then, as Martha hung back, she asked, 'What is it?'

'I'm afraid. All those people. I won't know who they are or what to say to them. And what about dinner. I'm sure I won't know how to eat half the dishes. Or what cutlery to use.'

'Martha!' Clarissa gave her a big hug. 'Fancy worrying about silly things like that. This isn't a big party. Just a few friends. It won't be stiff and formal. I'll sit near you and tell you who everyone is. And Matilda will be there – I'll ask her to keep an eye on you; just watch her. And keep thinking of old Lord Rossinver. He is always so busy talking that he usually picks up the wrong knife or fork – and then shouts at the footman for not putting it in the right place. As for talking, Mama says all a girl has to do is look pretty and smile. At least until she's married!'

Martha's first impression of the drawing-room was of lightness and elegance. Pale apricot walls with elaborate stucco mouldings. White ceiling. Golden-toned floor with a centre rug woven with pale-coloured wreaths of flowers. Small satin-covered chairs. Cabinets and tables inlaid in woods of different colours, with delicate legs. An ornate gilt clock on the marble mantelpiece.

'How beautiful!' she said involuntarily.

Lady Abigail, who was sitting near the fire, was pleased.

'You have a good eye. Refreshing in these days when people prefer to spend their money on horses and claret rather than on furniture . . . Now, let me look at the both of

you. Perfect! Aren't they, Merrion?'

'Eh, what, do speak up, Abigail.' Her husband held a hearing trumpet to his right ear. In a great wing armchair that looked a little out of scale compared to the rest of the furniture he looked broad and squat. He seemed a good deal older than Lady Abigail.

'Here is my god-daughter to meet you.' Lady Abigail spoke loudly into his trumpet as she drew Martha beside her. 'Dear Emily's daughter.'

'Well, 'pon my soul. Emily's daughter. 'Pon my soul. Come closer and let me see you, m'dear.'

Martha advanced and stood silently as Lord Merrion scrutinised her closely. 'Pretty, but not much family resemblance, is there?'

Martha's fears were renewed. Should she say something? Explain that it was all a mistake. But before she could utter a word, Lady Abigail broke in, 'Nonsense, Merrion. She is decidedly like Emily. Just look at her eyes, the turn of the head, that lovely long neck. Why, she's Emily to the life.'

'No reason why she shouldn't take after her father,' grumbled Merrion. 'But you're probably right . . . you usually are . . . the eyes are Emily's . . .'

Martha suspected that Lord Merrion fought a losing battle in family matters.

'I trust there wasn't any trouble from the rebels on your way here. I thought it was madness letting you come alone. What was your father thinking of? Females gadding round the country in these times.'

'But she wasn't on her own, Merrion.' Lady Abigail was beginning to sound a little impatient. 'She's been staying with the Montgomerys in Kells this past week, and their coachman and a groom drove her here today . . . Besides

Camden assures me that the restlessness is all over. They're handing in their arms . . . And, now, don't start on the subject this evening. At least not until we leave the drawing-room. There is nothing more boring than a cluster of men all trying to shout each other down about the state of the country.'

Martha smiled. Lord Merrion evidently was looking forward to war games – from an armchair. Once again, she wondered exactly what year it was. The French Revolution had been mentioned. That was 1789. The 'rebels' were a clue, but Irish history was littered with rebels. She decided she'd have to wait a little longer to solve the mystery. Then, with a start, she realised that Lord Merrion was talking to her.

'And how is Donegal? It's a long time since I have been there. Remember the salmon leap at Ballyshannon. Twelve feet high the falls were, a local man told me. And the bridge had fourteen arches . . . Ballyshannon is, of course, where the Conollys came from. Speaker Conolly was the son of a man who had a tavern there. His sister was married to Brigadier Henry Conyngham of Mountcharles who leased the fourteen ballyboes of church land in Killybegs.'

'Ballyboes? What may one ask, are "ballyboes",' Lady Abigail had an air of mounting impatience about her (that every hostess would have recognised) as she awaited the arrival of the first of the evening's guests.

'Don't know, m'dear. But Speaker Conolly got them in the end, they're still in the family . . .'

'I know,' said Martha unexpectedly, remembering old Master Diver at the National School talking about land. 'In olden days land was measured, not in acres, but by the number of cattle it could support. In Irish *báile bo*, hence ballyboes.'

'Now, Clarissa, do you hear that? . . . Martha you're a regular bluestocking! . . . Merrion, you haven't remarked, by the way, on how well Clarissa is looking this evening.'

'Very pretty, m'dear. Always like white on young girls. Hope you have a great party. Only pity is that your god-father won't be here to offer you felicitations. Strange fellow. There's an odd streak in those Kildares. And that daughter Lucy. I have it on first-hand information that she wanted to marry Arthur O'Connor. Fine marriage that would have been. He's now in jail awaiting trial.'

'Papa,' Clarissa went up to him and hugged him. 'Every family has its problems. Now, aren't you going to enjoy my birthday. Forget all these sad things.'

'You're right, m'dear.'

She glided away. There was a suppressed hint of excite-ment in her movements and her voice that puzzled Martha. Maybe in those days, birthdays were more special occasions than in her own age.

A footman threw open the door. 'Lord Andrew Morrison.'

Clarissa rushed over to him. 'Andrew! I'm glad you came early. You must meet my cousin Martha. Her birthday was yesterday, so this is really a joint celebration . . . Martha, this is Andrew, one of our very best friends. So you must like him.'

The young man smiled. Martha thought he looked rather dashing, with his slim upright figure, dark hair, and eyes that were now looking at her with admiration.

'I understand you just arrived today. . . You must think we are very sociable people in these parts. No sooner have you entered the front door than you find there is to be a party. With a ball tomorrow. Then the theatre. But I can assure you, Miss Martha, that this is most unusual. In the ordinary way, you would only find the family, dressed in their oldest clothes, grumbling to each other over a meagre fire, with Ramage serving up cold cuts from the breakfast table. Whereas you find the house ablaze with lights, a whole constellation of people in their best clothes, and the promise of a delicious dinner – and it will be delicious. I hear that Lord Clonmell lent Lady Abigail his two grand cooks. And here's Jonah Barrington to entertain us.'

'Which one is he?'

'The man who has just come in, with the rather large nose and the slightly scattered hair. He's a barrister, studied at Trinity – as I do now – and a member of Parliament. All in addition to being a famous teller of tall tales. They say the law produces great wits and great storytellers. I haven't found it so myself, but give me a decade or two. By the time I'm thirty-eight, I hope to have as many stories as Barrington.'

He had a light bantering tone of voice and when he smiled his eyes crinkled at the corners in a most engaging way. Very attractive, decided Martha.

The room was now filling up with people. Clarissa had come over again, breaking into the conversation with, 'You remember brother George and his wife Sophie? Sophie, our cousin Martha.'

George, a well set-up young man with blond hair a shade or two darker than Clarissa's, gave a half bow. He seemed rather stiff and formal. 'I would not have recognised you at all, Martha. You have changed since we last met.'

Martha hoped she would not be sitting beside him at dinner. He would be sure to ask her all kinds of awkward questions.

'Changed? Of course she has!' Sophie, a lively pretty woman who moved as nimbly as a bird, stepped forward and kissed Martha on both cheeks. 'She has grown up. And very prettily too. Pay no heed to Dunboyne. He never pays compliments.'

Andrew bent his head towards Martha and whispered, 'You will have noticed that the Cobbett family females always refer to their husbands by their titles. It sounds very affected but at least everyone knows to whom they are referring. Georges and Williams and Edwards abound in these circles.'

Ramage came in and approached Clarissa, saying something to her in a low voice. Her eyes lit up and she flew from the room. Andrew's eyes followed her as she left and he looked a little abstracted. Martha wondered if there was any special relationship with Clarissa, and for some odd reason she felt a pang of disappointment at the thought. Then she thought to herself, 'How silly! As if he could ever be anything to me.' But she did wonder why he was looking so serious. Perhaps someone had come in that he thought Clarissa should not meet and that Ramage had put him in the morning-room. But that was absurd. Everyone who came would have been invited by Lady Abigail.

'Who's that?' she asked, more in an effort to rekindle the conversation than for any other reason. She was not in the slightest interested in the latest entry – a stout, square man, dressed in dark clothes, whose thick coarse face was framed rather incongruously in dark curls.

Andrew frowned and said mechanically, 'McNally, Leonard McNally, another barrister.' Then his gloom seemed to lift. 'Odd fellow! They call him "one *pound* two".'

'Why on earth?'

'One leg is shorter than the other. So he takes one long stride with his good leg, and then two thumping steps with the other to bring them both level.'

At that moment Ramage announced dinner. As she swept past, Lady Abigail said to Andrew, 'Who asked that dreadful man? What makes him think he's welcome in Merrion Square, the defender of Napper Tandy and William Jackson. The man hasn't got a titter of sense. But . . .' 'Here comes the French Revolution,' whispered Clarissa, who had just come back into the drawing-room, to Martha. '. . . since the French Revolution everyone seems to think they have *carte blanche* to come and go as they please . . . Are you responsible, Andrew?'

'Heavens, no. I don't like the man. Maybe he came with Barrington.'

'Keep him at your end of the table and away from me.'

By this time Lord Merrion had managed, with some help, to rise from his armchair and join Lady Abigail to lead the way downstairs to the dining-room.

The dining room was just as magnificent as the drawing-room. The walls were pale blue, stucco panels framing paintings of landscapes, of men in uniform and ladies with romantic dresses against woodland trees. The ceiling had a circular garland of flowers, from which trailed leafy fronds and through which birds circled and flew. From the centre rose hung a glittering chandelier. Two tall curved windows, framed with white fluted columns, looked out on a garden at the back.

The long mahogany table was covered with a snowy white cloth and all the china, silver and crystal that Matilda had talked about. As Martha hesitated, Andrew beckoned her to a chair on his left; that on his right was reserved for Clarissa who slid in as the party was settling itself. Again, Martha felt that illogical pang of disappointment.

Matilda was opposite. She smiled at Martha and patted a fork. Clarissa had obviously been talking to her.

When they were seated, Martha looked around her, while whispered asides from Clarissa and Andrew filled in the guest list. Lady Abigail sat at the head of the far end of the table. 'Merrion should be sitting at our end but he prefers not to venture so far into the interior, so Charles takes his place. The man on the right of Matilda is Robert Latouche and on her right is Lord Crotty's son, William . . .' Clarissa gave a little blush as he was introduced. Maybe he was her

beau. 'Beside him is Lady Isabella Fitzgerald. The two girls on either side of George are Anne and Caroline, friends of Clarissa's.'He lowered his voice. 'The gigglers, I call them. They giggle about everything. Thank goodness you don't. You can't realise what a relief it is. The empty seat beside you will shortly be filled by Jonah Barrington. I told him to keep you entertained.'

Our end looks much livelier, thought Martha, as she glanced up the table. The seating arrangements hadn't quite worked out according to Lady's Abigail's specification. McNally was at her end of the table, and Martha pitied Sophie who was sandwiched in between him and a wintery-looking man who sat on Abigail's right. 'The Earl of Clifden,' explained Andrew. 'That's his wife opposite Sophie. They always sit within earshot of each other. He's up for the trial.'

Martha was about to ask what trial when Jonah Barrington took his seat beside her.

'Do I see my friend Colclough?' he asked looking up the table to his right.

'Cesar Colclough,' said Andrew to Martha. 'Son of Sir Vesey, brother of John. From Wexford.'

'You do indeed,' drawled Colclough.

'I saw your bother last month, at a dinner in Wexford. Harvey was there, asked me to go to Bargy Castle the following Monday to meet some old Temple friends of ours. An extraordinary gathering . . .'

Martha was trying to place the names. Bargy Castle? Harvey? But try as she could, her memory was blank. How provoking it all was! 'I'll pay more attention to history in future, and that's for sure,' she thought to herself.

'Why did you look so worried there?' asked Andrew who had been carrying on a conversation with Clarissa and William. 'You look so much prettier when you smile.'

Meanwhile food was being placed before Martha in

astonishing profusion by Ramage and his retinue of footmen – soup, boiled chicken, turbot, sole and vegetables.
Martha noted in surprise that there were almost as many
servants as guests.

'A toast to Clarissa,' said Lord Merrion. Their glasses
were filled with champagne and they raised them to each
other before drinking. 'Now, Lady Abigail,' and she too
raised her glass and drank the toast.

In the confusion of glasses being raised and names called,
Martha must have looked puzzled because Andrew said,
'The toast goes round the table. First to the lady you want
to drink to, then to the hostess and the host and then to
every other guest.'

'You will drink a toast with me,' said Barrington to
Martha. 'To the sixteenth of May.'

'Your birthday! What a pretty idea,' smiled Andrew.

As glasses were filled and refilled, Martha couldn't help
saying, 'What a lot everyone drinks.'

'They say that in England many people with a thousand a
year never drink wine, while here even those with a hundred
a year drink freely.'

'There's a neat story about that,' put in Barrington. 'In
England they talk about wine stands . . . here we call them
coasters. I was recently taken to task by an Englishman who
insisted on the word "stand". "Ah, but," I said to him, "in
Ireland the wine rarely stands" . . . but to go back to Harvey
and Bargy Castle . . . that strange gathering . . .'

McNally was looking up from his end of the table but
such was the hum of conversation that Martha doubted
that he could hear anything. Especially as Sophie had to
raise her voice to talk to old Lady Clifden. 'Cousin of mine
was there, Captain Keogh, and as the night wore on, our
discussion got quite heated. The subject was Irish politics.
The distracted state of the country. The probability of a
speedy revolt. The government severities. The chances of

success, in the event of a rising. All very circumspect.
Arguments highly hypothetical. But there was something in
the tone that made me uneasy . . .

'I decided to turn the talk on its head and make a joke of
the subject. "My dear Keogh," I said jestingly, "it is quite
clear that you and I, in this famous rebellion, shall be on
different sides of the question; and of course one or the
other of us must necessarily be hanged at or before its ter-
mination – I upon a lamp-iron in Dublin, or you on the
bridge of Wexford. Now, we'll make a bargain! If we beat
you, upon my honour, I'll do all I can to save your neck;
and if your folks beat us, you'll save me from the honour of
the lamp-iron." '

All the dishes from the first course had been cleared and
a magnificent salmon was placed at the end of the table,
before George. The footmen rushed around with dishes of
beans, potatoes, peas and salads.

'Do you go the Viceregal Lodge tomorrow night, Miss
Martha,' asked William.

'I believe so. Lady Abigail mentioned it.'

'I understand we're to put on some sort of entertainment,' put in Robert.

'How exciting!' said Martha. 'Will you take part?' she
asked Andrew.

'I've been bespoke by Clarissa. Most of her friends here
will also take part . . . and, depend on it . . . you'll have to
join in too.'

'But I couldn't.'

'It'll be so simple,' said Clarissa, 'you can't imagine.
We're to have a rehearsal after dinner.'

'Someone was talking about Lady Antrim's famous "bal-
let" of a few years ago and Lady Abigail undertook to
arrange a still more splendid entertainment,' said Andrew.
'We are to out-perform those brilliant ladies of Grand Scots
fame with a dance, the shape of which has not yet been

decided and the steps of which are still a mystery.'

The salmon being removed, the next course arrived – rabbit and onions, veal and olives, lobster fricassée, lamb ragôut . . . Claret had succeeded the champagne and the toasts were flying fast and furious.

'A toast,' called Barrington. 'To the glorious – pious – and immortal memory of the great and good King William; not forgetting Oliver Cromwell, who assisted in redeeming us from popery, slavery, arbitrary power, brass-money and wooden shoes.'

'And another,' from Colclough. 'To the memory of the chestnut horse.'

'That broke King William's neck,' said Andrew with a smile.

'I don't know about the horse,' said Barrington. 'It

would seem ungracious to toast the animal that broke our benefactor's neck.'

'How was that?' asked Martha.

'Our family dates from James the First. Cromwell confirmed our grant, but William preserved it.'

'We know,' said George somewhat wearily.

But Barrington was not to be diverted. 'Naturally, when James the Second came along, those who weren't with him were against him. So my ancestor, Colonel John Barrington, was ousted from his estates by a Jacobite wig-maker. Peacefully, it must be said, with a promise of £40 a year if he behaved himself.

'Two months later he repossessed himself of his mansion. The wig-maker complained to Dublin and a party of soldiers was sent down to sort out Colonel John. Which they did in the most expeditious way, ordering that he be hanged within the hour.

'The execution was to be carried out on the cross bar of his own gate. Picture the dramatic scene! The Colonel, the wig-maker, the old retainers desolate, the Jacobites in triumph.

'But just as the first haul was given to elevate him, a tenant of the estate, Ned Doran, a trooper in the army of James the Second, rode up, himself and horse in a state of complete exhaustion.

' "Holloa, Holloa," he shouted. "Cut down the Colonel. Cut down the Colonel. Or ye'll all be hanged. I am straight from the Boyne water. We're all cut up and kilt to the devil and back again. Jemmy's scampered."

'Everyone disappeared. Ned Doran cut him down and fell on his knees to beg pardon of his landlord, the holy Virgin and King William from the Boyne water.

'So that, in short, is how our estates were saved. So I'll drink to King William . . .'

'How strange,' thought Martha to herself. 'Cromwell and

King William! Wouldn't I cause a sensation if I responded to the toast of the chestnut horse!'

Barrington turned to Martha, 'I must tell you about a curious club of which I was at one time a member, The Aldermen of Skinners' Abbey. It was started by aldermen who had been deposed by King James. On being restored by King William they formed a club and had a big celebrations on the first of July, the anniversary of the battle of the Boyne. The charter-dish was sheeps' trotters . . .'

'Barrington,' called George. 'Do you go to the Kingston trial tomorrow?'

'Sheeps' trotters,' queried Martha.

'In memory of King James running away.'

The main part of dinner now being concluded, the various dishes and the tablecloth were removed, exposing the mahogany table top in all its highly polished splendour. In a very short time it was covered with china baskets of candied and preserved fruit, silver comports piled high with hot-house fruits, glasses of sparkling jellies, creams, ices and orange pudding, cheese-cakes, strawberries served on fluted silver dishes, cream and apple pie. Small plates of olives, sweetmeats and nuts completed the array.

'I just couldn't eat another bite,' groaned Martha (who had, in fact, being unused to such quantities of food, eaten very sparingly).

'Do you think Lord Kingston will be convicted?' asked William.

'I gather his plea is self-defence,' said Barrington. 'Said he thought his half-brother was a United Irishman.'

Lady Abigail evidently thought the conversation was about to take a political turn for very shortly she gave the signal for the ladies to withdraw. As Martha rose, Andrew bowed. 'I'll be in the drawing-room in half an hour.'

Outside, on the landing, Clarissa, Isabella and Caroline, heads together, were giggling.

'Did you see him?'

'I vow, I wouldn't have known him.'

'Clarissa, did you know he was coming?'

'Well, he *is* my godfather and he knew it was my birthday.'

When Martha went to her bedroom, Breege was there and the commode was uncovered.

'How do the gentlemen manage?'

'Some go into the garden.' Breege smiled. 'And there's a room downstairs. Full of chamber-pots. Dozens of them. Takes Marty half a night to empty them all into the cesspit.'

'Probably all more civilised than the dreadful outdoor toilets that were still the norm in rural Ireland in the 1940s,' decided Martha.

As Martha descended the stairs again, she was trying to coordinate the bits of information that had come her way so far. It was like piecing a jigsaw together.

It was definitely the era of the United Irishmen. The country had been in a state of unrest but now all was calm. Or was it? What did Jonah Barrington means by saying that talk of revolt was hypothetical? It could be 1792. Or 1795. Or – she felt a twinge of unease – 1798?

'I'll find some way of checking tonight,' she thought. 'But how on earth do I do that? I can hardly ask what year it is. But, of course, there must be newspapers. How do I get hold of one? "Bluestocking" Martha wants to see the *Daily News* or whatever they had in those days. There must be other ways of finding out the year. Not with calendars – what was the word? Almanacks! That was it. She would ask Breege for one that very night.

Suddenly she was aware of voices on the landing outside the drawing-room.

'Of all the ill-considered things!'

'He sent a message. With Lanigan. That he'd be here. I couldn't have stopped him.'

'We'll have to get him out immediately. I heard McNally expressing a wish to see the ceiling of the morning-room.'

'We'll just say no.'

'He might suspect something. A careless word dropped in a receptive ear could be disastrous. Not only for him but for people here. There are informers everywhere.'

When Martha reached the turn of the stairs, Clarissa had vanished. Andrew took her hand. 'You must help. Something that could have terrible consequences has happened. Go into the drawing-room. You'll find McNally there – the only gentleman to surface. There's something afoot. Keep him in conversation. Don't let him leave the room. Give us ten minutes.'

He turned abruptly and went down the stairs to the morning-room.

Martha, heart aflutter, went into the drawing-room. Lady Abigail was sitting by the fireplace where, even on this fine evening, a fire blazed. On a table nearby tea and coffee services were laid out. McNally was standing by one of the long windows that looked out on to the greenery of Merrion Square. He was talking to Sophie.

'I believe the ceiling in the morning-room is the greatest achievement of Robert West. I should be deeply indebted if you would allow me to see it.'

'Of course.' Sophie was at a loss for words. Lady Abigail muttered, 'Half-mounted gentlemen. Come uninvited to dinner – and want to see over the house.'

'Let me talk to him,' Martha said, and went over to McNally. How on earth could she detain him for ten minutes.

Smiling as sweetly as she could she said, 'The ceilings here are so beautiful, are they not?'

'Commonly admitted, Miss . . . Martha . . . is it?'

'Yes, Martha.' She frantically cast around in her mind for instances of the glories of Georgian Dublin. All she could remember was the chapel of the Rotunda. 'I understand it's even more magnificent.'

'Quite.' he gave a slight bow, and, shortened leg in evidence, was preparing to stomp away when she circumvented him.

'You are a friend of Jonah Barrington, are you not?'

'We are both barristers. That is true.'

'He said something at dinner, that some shot he fired was your salvation. He didn't finish the story.'

'You have the advantage of me there, Miss. I don't seem to remember any such circumstance.' He was edging away again.

'I believe you are a playwright as well as being a barrister.'

'Ah, you are interested in the theatre. You like the performances at Smock Alley?'

'Very much. What do you think of them yourself?'

'It is quite some time since I had the pleasure of attending there . . . the theatre closed down eleven years ago.'

Martha was stung into attack. 'You don't much like them, do you?'

'Who?'

'The Cobbetts, the Crottys, the Dunboynes.'

He looked at her and came to a standstill. 'You express yourself very forcibly for a young lady. And why, pray, should I not like them?'

'I saw it tonight, at dinner. You seldom spoke. You looked at them with . . . a sort of envy, I thought.'

'Hmm . . . I used to think cross-examination was my forte. But you're right, however wrongly your conclusion was reached. Often I don't speak. Not because I'm short of conversation but because I prefer to listen. One learns more by listening to other people's voices than to one's own . . . It's true I don't like them.'

'Why? They seem to me to be so high-spirited, so full of charm, so gallant . . .'

'They are fools. When they are young they are blind fools. Playing at war, on one side or another. Lord Edward, before he went into hiding, was wont to strut up Kildare Street dressed in French fashion, hair cropped short. He thinks he is untouchable because of his connections. Wolfe Tone thought he could bring down the British government by going to France with a hundred guineas in his pocket.

'And when they are old, they grow stupid, fuddled by memories of lost causes and forgotten wars. And who suffers? We do. Caught in the middle of all this. Well, we have our escape routes. I have the law. You, judging by tonight, have captured the heart of Andrew Morrison.'

Martha blushed and as she turned away, she caught sight of Andrew at the door. He nodded. After a whispered word, Sophie tripped over. 'I believe you expressed a wish to see the morning-room.'

McNally smiled sardonically. 'Another time, perhaps.'

He bowed to Martha and stomped away, neglecting to take his leave of Lady Abigail, a fact duly noted for comment.

'What was all that about?' Martha asked Andrew.

'I'll tell you later. Now, Clarissa wants us all inside.'

4 The Ländler

The drawing-room was L-shaped: a long room with two windows overlooking the square, and a smaller room, half the width, with another huge window which looked out to the small rear garden and the stables. The two parts were divided by folding doors. Ramage was in the process of closing one half of the door.

The young people, having collected tea or coffee cups from the table in the main room, had assembled in the garden part.

'We must finally decide what we're going to do,' Clarissa was saying. 'We've already had two rehearsals and nobody has thought of anything.'

'The minuet,' came from Caroline.

'We're all sick and tired of the minuet. Anyway, tomorrow it's going to be 'No swords and no hoops.' You can't have have a real minuet without hoops.'

'What about the *allemande*?' said Lady Isabella Fitzgerald. 'I remember we had such fun at Carton dancing it with Uncle Eddy.' Her eyes clouded over momentarily. 'Or what about an Irish jig. He is very fond of Irish jigs – someone said he is a "famous hand" at them. We used to have a piper to play for us.'

'What about the minuet?' said William again.

The conversation rambled on. There was more tea and more coffee.

'What ditherers!' thought Martha. Forgetting her initial

awe at being in the presence of descendants of dukes and earls, she spoke up:

'Why don't we dance . . .' everyone looked at her, '. . . the ländler? It's all the thing in Austria at the moment.'

'The ländler?' It seemed nobody had ever heard of the ländler. But they were all enthusiasm to try something new.

'Now, let me see. It's danced to this kind of music.' Martha sat down at the piano in the corner and played a Schubert ländler. 'No point in telling them it hasn't yet been composed,' she thought, as she played the old familiar air beloved of Frau Hassler.

'I think I've got the air.' Matilda came over and sat down at the piano. 'You tell them how to dance it.'

'Let's get Danny,' said Clarissa. 'He plays the fiddle.'

In no time at all Matilda and Danny produced a very creditable rendering of Schubert and Martha tried to instruct the eight dancers in a dance of which she had only a vague idea. But she had always been good at dancing, particularly Irish sets, and, comforting herself with the thought that nobody would have a yardstick with which to measure performance, she set to to devise a set of figures based on the rhythm and Frau Hassler's memories.

'Now, one-two-three, sway, turn. One-two-three, dip, bend. Cross over arms, one-two-three. Now arms behind your backs, one-two-three.'

The germ of a dance pattern was beginning to emerge. William was hopeless, always getting his feet mixed up. Clarissa took everything at too fast a pace. Anne kept looking at the ground, and Colclough tended to pause in mid-step, ear cocked, to listen to the conversation drifting out from the drawing-room.

'Look up, smile.' Martha could hear the voice of Frau Hassler. 'Nobody's going to look at your feet. Whatever mistakes you make, look up, head erect, shoulders back, and smile. Throw your head back. Enjoy yourself!'

'Phew, let's have a rest,' pleaded William after a while. 'Out of condition since the hunting stopped.'

Martha and Andrew sat near the half-open folding door and as the footman came round with tea and coffee she listened with half an ear to the voices inside.

'The great mistake was Abercrombie. What Commander-in-Chief would so revile his troops as to say, "Disgraceful . . . formidable to everyone but the enemy."? Man should be court martialled.'

'Well, he was forced to resign, wasn't he? General Lake is the man for dealing with rebels.'

'By flogging them? Burning their wretched hovels? Half hanging them? Pitch-capping them? The use of torture seems to me more likely to turn honest folk into rebels.' Lady Abigail's voice was frosty. Martha could imagine her annoyance that the evening had, after all, turned into a political discussion.

'Mama, you don't understand.' That sounded like George. 'The south was in absolute rebellion. Attacks in broad daylight. Arms being taken. Landlords murdered in their beds. Martial law had to be imposed. If there is a fire it must be stamped out.'

'Lady Abigail, and gentlemen,' the soothing voice must belong to Jonah Barrington, 'let us not get too heated. England, of course, means very well. But do you really imagine she has any interest in us? We're a colony. To be exploited.'

'I think Prime Minister Pitt did his best. He promised reforms. He sent Fitzwilliam over as Viceroy.'

'And brought him back on the next boat.'

'Fitzwilliam was a fool. He shouldn't have tried to get rid of Beresford.'

'But how could he put through reforms without removing the men who would have opposed them?'

'Barrington,' the testy voice of Lord Merrion asked, 'do

you side with the Napper Tandys, the Wolfe Tones, the Lord Edwards, the wild revolutionaries?'

'Lord Merrion, I'm an advocate. I merely advance arguments – on one side or the other. *I* take no sides. I just ask you to consider whether there might not be cause for all the dissatisfaction. We were all united for liberty in the days of the Volunteers.'

'That was sixteen years ago.'

'Have ideals changed in those years?'

'They have got into the wrong hands,' said George stiffly.

'I have met Wolfe Tone. Useless at the Bar. I took him around myself in my carriage three times but I could see he would never grasp the science of the law. But an open honest fellow, with the highest principles.'

'Liberty, equality and fraternity!'

'Much the same sentiments as the Volunteers expressed – only maybe not so pithily . . . I knew Lord Edward too. Impetuous. Too little used to thinking. But a man of absolute integrity.'

'Meaning what?' growled Lord Merrion.

'Contrast two sides of the coin:

'On one two faces: A man with a price on his head, and an exile in France, knowing that if he returns he will face a charge of high treason. Yet I would be more than happy to take my chance with either of them as judge.

'On the other side, three faces: John Fitzgibbon, son of a man who was destined for the Catholic church, who changed his religion and adopted law; John Scott, who rose into the air as precipitously as a lark, building his fortune by holding lands for Catholics – who, as you know, could not hold them – and then dishonouring the agreements; and John Beresford who only thinks only of power and money.

'While the hangman awaits the men of principle, the others have become earls, like Fitzgibbon and Scott, or rich like Beresford . . .

'I speak, of course, only as an advocate. It is all purely hypothetical . . .'

'I hope he's got that point across,' said Andrew. 'Or else old Clifden, who's slow on the uptake, will have him marked down as an United Irishman and that could be a trifle inconvenient.'

Clarissa came rushing up. 'Now just one more rehearsal.'

Outside in the gathering twilight dusk was beginning to fall. A pale crescent moon was emerging through thin spring leaves.

'Let's go into the garden,' said Clarissa.

They went down to the dining-room where the servants were clearing away the remains of the feast, and through the open window into the garden.

'What happens to everything?' asked Martha, thinking of the gargantuan quantities of food.

'The servants get it,' said Matilda. 'They may have long hours but here they feast on the fat of the land.'

In the garden the air was cool and fresh, fragrant with flowers and shrubs. One scent above all others filled the air – the scent of the lilacs. Andrew picked a sprig and presented it to Martha.

'To the girl with the violet eyes,' he said.

And Martha, who knew her eyes were not violet, did not argue. She smiled up at him, remembering the touch of his hand, the laughter in his eyes, the warmth of his smile. The fragrance of the lilacs, the young May moon, the soft darkness of the night, came together to create an atmosphere in which dull reality was suspended and banished.

When she went up to bed, Breege was sitting by the fire.

'Oh, Breege, you shouldn't have waited up for me.'

'But of course, Miss Martha. I must be here when you come to bed.'

'And can you sleep in the morning?'

'Up at cockcrow,' replied Breege cheerfully. 'Now into bed with you. It'll be a long day tomorrow.'

As she put on the tucked nightgown, warm from being heated before the fire, Martha asked, 'What was happening in the morning-room tonight?' Servants, she figured, must know everything that happened in the house.

'Nothing that I know of, Miss.'

'I thought there was someone concealed there . . . and Clarissa and Andrew Morrison were trying to get him or her away before Lady Abigail found out.'

Breege looked at her blankly. 'I don't know, Miss. Nobody spoke about it downstairs.'

'You mean you're not telling,' thought Martha. Then as she lay back in bed she decided it was really no business of hers. Tomorrow she would go to the ball that the ruby ring had promised her. Afterwards she would twist the ring, make a wish and be back in 1944, in Donegal. She'd worry about explaining the missing day to her parents later on.

As for Andrew, was there something going on between him and Clarissa? Why did the thought hurt?

As she got into bed she remembered the almanack.

'Breege, I don't have my almanack with me. And with all the travelling, I've got so confused that I don't know what day it is. Is there one around anywhere?'

Breege went away and returned with a decorative card. 'Here you are – and here we are. The seventeenth of May.'

With fast-beating heart, Martha looked at the top of the card. The date was 1798.

As she fell asleep, the nostalgic echo of the ländler floated through her dreams, to be replaced, menacingly, with the stomp, stomp, stomp of McNally's leg.

5   Muslin – and Drama

Next morning Martha awoke to see the smiling face of Breege bent over her.

'I have brought you a cup of hot chocolate, Miss Martha. Breakfast is not until ten o'clock.'

Having drunk her chocolate, Martha climbed out of bed and went to the window. The curtains were drawn back and bright sunlight flooded in. Across the street, the shrubs and trees in the square, showing the pale green of young growth, blotted out all evidence of a city beyond. There was nobody about except a man in rough shirt and trousers who was leading a horse and cart on which stood a very large wooden barrel. He seemed to be stopping at every house. Breege explained that he was delivering water, which was stored in the basement.

'We're back in the days before piped water!' Martha decided. She shivered slightly as she turned from the window, and stared at the ruby ring on her finger. Its deep warm glow reassured her. All would be well.

She stood behind the painted screen and quickly washed herself, grateful that the water was warm, even though there was so little of it. She could now understand why, having seen the water cart.

Breege had laid out a striped muslin dress, cream silk stockings embroidered with clocks, and green leather shoes with low heels and pointed toes. Having dressed, Martha moved to the dressing-table to have her hair done. When she thought of her usual morning routine, which consisted of splashing cold water on her face and running a comb through her hair, she had to smile.

The family were already at breakfast when she arrived in the breakfast-room. The table was laden with silver dishes containing warm rolls, muffins, toast, butter, honey, all kinds of bread, even spiced buns, and small cakes. Lady Abigail presided over the tea and coffee pots, though hot chocolate was also on offer.

When they had finished eating, Lady Abigail said briskly, 'Now, we have no time to lose. I've ordered the carriage for eleven. Meanwhile, Martha, we'll go up and see what you have brought with you.'

As Lady Abigail sorted the contents of the travelling trunks into two piles, briskly separating the 'sheep' from the 'goats', Martha stood by in silence. A strange protective feeling came over her as she watched the clothes of the stranger whose name she was usurping, come under detailed scrutiny.

The nightgowns, frilled night caps, and negligées were put on the sheeps' side; the goats' selection mounted alarmingly.

'Tabinet, black? Mourning at your age! Hm, a pretty colour,' holding up a parchment-coloured sarsanet, 'but the set of those sleeves is horrible. Dark-blue calico – m'dear, you'll look like an ink-blot . . .' They all joined the goats. Three were retained, with the promise that new trimmings would make new gowns of them. The hats were to undergo similar treatment.

At first Martha raged inwardly at the rejection of her wardrobe. But Clarissa and Matilda were in paroxysms of laughter and suddenly she saw the funny side of it. The country cousin come to conquer the capital in dark-blue calico, black tabinet and purple satin. She thought of the beautiful dress she had worn the evening before and joined in the laughter.

'I really must speak to your father,' concluded Lady Abigail as she swept from the room. 'But now we must get you something suitable for tonight.'

'Where are we going?' asked Martha.

'Foleys in Capel Street. The Court dressmakers. They have the *very* latest fashions.'

Putting on hats and spencers, they descended to the hall. The door was open and Joseph, eye-catching in blue and gold, was handing Lady Abigail into the carriage. Martha managed without the helping hand which, she noted, Clarissa and Matilda seemed to take for granted.

As they clattered through the streets, Lady Abigail, who was wearing a ferocious-looking bonnet with ostrich feathers, called out the sights. 'Trinity College – founded in 1591. Provost's house – must remember them for our next dinner. Houses of Parliament – have to get back in time for the trial. Carlisle Bridge – can't think why they built it. Sackville Street – so much more elegant when it was Gardiner's Mall.'

As they turned into Henry Street, Martha became aware of a commotion outside the carriage. Darting out from the narrow dark alleyways that led off the street were countless ragged children, running from the ramshackle mud cabins in the lanes. They swarmed alongside the carriage, thin brown arms caked in filth outstretched, emaciated bodies barely covered with rags, feet bare except for the covering of mud and dust. They were calling, 'God bless yer ladyship,' over and over again, pinched faces upraised and smiling, showing mouthfuls of decaying teeth.

Martha recoiled in horror but Lady Abigail, with a sigh, took out a stocking purse and tossed some coins out of the carriage window. A howl went up as the children dived for them, the older and stronger kicking away the weaker. The

contrast between the lavishness of the dinner last night and
the poverty on the streets today was so striking that Martha
wondered at the almost complete indifference displayed by
Clarissa and Matilda. They were chatting quietly to each
other, the only acknowledgement of the scene outside being
an urgent request from Clarissa to have the window put up
quickly as the stench was so intolerable.

'Drive on, Joseph,' ordered Lady Abigail, and scattering
children and dogs alike they continued down the street.

'I can see you are shocked, Martha,' said Lady Abigail.
But surely there is poverty in Donegal too . . .'

'Yes, but . . .' Martha didn't quite know what to say but
luckily Lady Abigail was in full flight.

'I know, I know. So much splendour on the one hand, so
much poverty and suffering on the other. I don't know what
the answer is, I'm sure. They crowd into the cities – where
there is no work for them to do. The only way they can live
is by begging or stealing. And there are so many of them ...'

They passed by a premises which was so beautifully lit up
with cut-glass chandeliers and lights that Martha thought it
must be a glass show-rooms. The interior, papered in green
and gold, was crowded with ragged men, women and children. Lady Abigail sighed.

'That's one reason why the poor stay poor. The lottery.
Run by the government. They take the pennies of the poor
to put it into the pockets of people like the Beresfords.'

'But how can those people afford to buy tickets?'

'They can't. A ticket costs about five pounds. But you
can lay a wager with an office clerk in any lottery office –
and believe me, every street is full of them – that a certain
number will be drawn. Those miserable wretches are in
there bartering the shillings that should be buying bread, for
the chance of making a few pounds. They hold the draw in
a hall in Capel Street. I attended one such "Wheel of
Fortune" and never did I see naked misery. Such shrieking.

Such weeping. Such lamentations. It doesn't bear thinking about . . .'

'See, there is Foleys,' said Matilda, pointing to a large bow window with quaint-looking leaded windows through which one could catch glimpses of colourful materials. A discreet notice just inside the shop door announced, 'Castle Dresses. From 5 guineas to 10 guineas.'

Lady Abigail was obviously a most important client, because the chief assistant, who had been waiting on another customer, handed her over immediately to an underling and came across, with a gushing, 'So nice to see your ladyship again.'

'A ballgown for my god-daughter.'

The assistant bowed and led the way to the back of the shop where they inspected the array of dresses. Lady Abigail was nothing if not decided and Martha cast an anguished glance at Clarissa as two models caught her eye.

First a pink clouded tabinet with a white petticoat, liberally trimmed with silver. Then a blue brocade over a white satin slip, with a train of blue satin edged with festoons of tulle and satin.

At this point the assistant, who had so far maintained a diplomatic silence, brought out a filmy pale-yellow sprigged muslin and Martha fitted it on.

'Not quite what I had in mind,' said Lady Abigail. 'Not really grand enough for a viceregal ball. But, child, it's perfect on you. I must resist the impulse to turn a wildflower into a hothouse gardenia.'

Martha could have hugged her. She felt so at ease in the fluid lines of the yellow muslin whereas the other dresses had seemed uncomfortably formal and rigid, making her feel like a child dressed in adult clothes.

'Now a pair of matching slippers. Some ostrich feathers? Perhaps not. We don't want to spoil the ship with a penny's worth of tar. Now a slip. What colour should it be?'

There was a brief discussion on the merits of white or a pale cream, the latter winning the day.

Back in Merrion Square, Joseph gave the large flat box, which had been tied with a white satin ribbon, to Ramage, who conveyed it to a footman, who brought it upstairs to Breege, who unpacked it with cries of ecstasy.

'Oh, Miss Martha, you'll be the belle of the ball. I'm sure of it. Such a lovely dress. And see,' putting the slip beneath it, 'how the cream brings up the delicate colour.'

Martha had to smile. Lady Abigail might sigh for the court dresses of yesteryear. Breege was all for the new.

She had barely time to take off her hat and have her hair (disturbed by the fitting-on) tidied before Clarissa came in.

'Do hurry. The carriage is waiting.'

'Where are we going now?'

'The House of Commons, for the Kingston trial. It's a

bore, really. On such a beautiful day. I wanted to take you
to the Rotunda gardens, but Papa has to be there and
Mama says we must go as there hasn't been a trial like this
for fifty years.'

'It was mentioned last night. Whose trial is it?'

'Lord Kingston.'

By this time they were downstairs and Joseph was waiting
with the carriage. Lord Merrion was resplendent in crimson
velvet, brocade waistcoat, laced ruffles and a powdered wig.
His legs, below his breeches, were encased in silk stockings
embroidered with gold clocks. His buckled shoes appeared
to be giving him some trouble because as he hobbled to the
carriage, he was heard to mutter, 'Demned uncomfortable.
Pinching like the devil. Throw them out tomorrow.' But
that was in the future. Meanwhile he had to suffer.

Lady Abigail was almost as splendid, in a heavily embroidered satin bodice and an overskirt of velvet.

'Everyone talks about Lord Kingston,' said Martha. 'Who
is he?'

'A peer of the realm,' grunted Lord Merrion. 'Has to be
tried by his fellow peers.'

'That's Papa,' said Clarissa.

'Well, he wasn't a peer at the time of the crime.' Lady
Abigail spoke loudly for her husband's benefit.

'Really, this is getting like twenty questions,' thought
Martha. 'Am I ever going to find out about Lord Kingston?'

'What actually happened?' she said aloud.

'His daughter was seduced by his half-brother,' said Lady
Abigail. 'So he shot him.'

'Not the whole story,' said Lord Merrion. 'Kingston
thought he was being attacked by a United Irishman. So he
fired. Turned out he had shot his half-brother.'

Lady Abigail gave a slight snort of derision. 'I don't see
he has to justify himself. Can't think what he is being tried
for. Surely he has the right to avenge his daughter.'

'Not according to the law, m'dear.'

'Why is this the first such trial for fifty years?' asked Martha.

'Because peers rarely commit crimes,' explained Lady Abigail drily. 'Duelling is a much simpler way of settling matters . . . Why didn't Kingston send him a challenge?'

'Might have been killed himself. At least he made sure of his man.'

'Is duelling not against the law?' said Martha.

'Well, if it is someone should tell the Bench. Who's going to proceed against the Lord Chancellor, Earl Clare? Fought a duel with Curran. Or Lord Clonmell because he called out a Privy Counsellor? And what about Chief Justice Paterson? Three duels, one with swords, another with guns. Wounded his man every time.'

'Barrington says it's an honest way of slaughtering someone – as no one knows who is the one to be slaughtered. Thank heavens,' Lady Abigail raised her eyes, 'that George has more sense than to go around blazing.'

'But it does give rise to some splendid stories,' put in Clarissa. 'Remember Curran and Egan? Egan said it was an unfair contest as there was so much more of him that he offered a better target. So Curran proposed that his outline be chalked on Egan – only shots within this target area to count!'

Lord Merrion was still unravelling the complexities of the case. 'The crime was committed when Kingston was Colonel Kingston. Then his father died and he became Lord Kingston. Hence the trial.'

Martha was amused. No fuss about an 'alleged' murder. And a judge willing to discuss the case with his family!

Martha was very interested to see the inside of the House of Commons, which had been chosen in preference to the House of Lords as it was much larger. The room was a perfect rotunda, with Ionic pilasters. A gallery, supported by columns divided into compartments, had space for seven hundred spectators, all with an uninterrupted view of the chamber. Above rose the cupola, its immense height dwarfing the participants in this archaic drama.

The front row of the gallery had been reserved for ladies of rank, and one compartment, covered with scarlet cloth, for peeresses and their daughters. Lady Abigail secured a front seat, and flanked by Clarissa and Martha, looked around her, raising pearl-handled opera glasses to her eyes.

'Who's here?' asked Martha.

'Just about everybody. That's Lady Clonmell in the white satin with diamonds – they say her husband is at death's door. Lady Clare – what an enormous turban, wonder anyone behind her can see anything. Lady Moira – did you know her late husband married three times, each time to a daughter of an earl? Lady Aldborough . . .'

'They say she built Aldborough House because she and the earl couldn't live in the same house.'

'I have heard it said that her tongue is like steel, the edge of her wit so keen and polished that the patient is never mangled; just cut to pieces . . . However, I understand that the earl's house in Denmark Street is entailed and as she has no children, she can't inherit. Now at least she'll have Aldborough House . . .'

There was a slight stir. The great doors at the end of the chamber were thrown open by liveried footmen, and led by the Lord Chancellor there entered the seventy-one peers, each carrying a white wand, in full dress and robed according to rank. As they took their seats, the Lord Chancellor in the Speaker's chair, the silence was so profound that one could have heard a pin drop. The chatter from the galleries was hushed and all eyes were on the door through which the prisoner would enter.

He was preceeded by Sir Chichester Fortescue, the King-at-Arms, who carried an emblazoned shield with the armorial bearings of the accused man. He placed himself to the left of the bar. Then came the moment for which everyone was waiting, the arrival of Lord Kingston. He was dressed in deep mourning and moved with a slow and melancholy step, his eyes fixed on the ground. He walked up to the bar and stood beside the King-at-Arms who held his armorial shield on a level with his shoulder.

The executioner next approached, bearing a large hatchet with an immense broad blade, painted black except for the two inches at the edge which were bright polished steel. He placed himself at the bar to the right of the prisoner, raising the hatchet almost as high as Lord Kingston's neck but with the shining edge turned away.

'If he is found guilty, the edge of the blade will be turned towards his neck,' explained Lady Abigail. Martha shuddered. It was unbelievable that this was all happening before her very eyes.

The prisoner knelt while the charge was read. He pleaded not guilty and the trial proceeded.

'Let anyone who can give evidence against the noble prisoner come forward,' proclaimed a court official. There was a deadly hush. The proclamation was made again, this time naming the peers. As each name was called a rustle of excitement ran through the crowd. Heads were turned, necks craned, to see if anyone was about to come forward. The slightest movement in the peers' compartment was eyed with anxiety and interest. The suspense was tangible.

Three times the names were called but not one peer appeared at the bar.

The official then declared. 'No witnesses appearing to substantiate the charge of murder against Robert, Earl of Kingston, the trial shall terminate in the accustomed manner.'

Lord Clare then asked, 'Guilty or not Guilty,' and one by

one, according to rank, the peers walked by the chair in which he was seated and placing his hand solemnly on his heart declared, 'Not guilty, upon my honour.'

This ceremony occupied an hour, after which the Chancellor rose and declared the opinion of the Peers of Ireland – 'That Robert, Earl of Kingston, is not guilty of the charge against him.' He then broke his wand, descended from the chair and thus ended the trial.

Martha had seen Andrew in the galleries. He waved to her but did not come over.

'He's attending his father,' said Lady Abigail, 'who shouldn't be here at all. Weak heart. This rigmarole of a trial is going to cause the deaths of half the peers of Ireland. Well, you'll see him tonight.'

But suddenly Andrew was beside them.

'Lady Abigail, you must go home immediately. Don't linger here.'

'Why ever not? Andrew, you're being most mysterious. I was promising myself a chat with Lady Leitrim and Mrs Craig. Explain yourself.'

'Don't ask me why, but, please, leave here as soon as possible.'

Seeing that she was still unconvinced, he added, 'I had it from Barrington just now. There's a rumour afoot that some sort of coup has been planned. That there is an assassination list. And could there be a better opportunity than now, with the Lord Chancellor, the Lord Chief Justice, the Speaker, the judges, the peers and the aristocracy all gathered here. In God's name, go.'

Somewhat unwillingly, Lady Abigail sent a messenger in search of Lord Merrion and a footman was dispatched to fetch the carriage. As they waited beneath the massive doors, she said pettishly, 'What an age we live in! Nothing but rumour and counter rumour. And not a word of it true,

I'll be bound. It's too bad of Andrew. I always thought of him as a rational young man. And yet here he is, giving ear to every tittle of gossip that that fool Barrington feeds him. If we were to believe everything we hear, we would have been murdered in our beds long since . . . Talking of which I meant to point out Sir Boyle Roche to you – the man who declared, in this very House, that if the murderous French republicans broke in, they would cut us to mince meat and throw our bleeding heads upon the table, to stare us in the face.'

McNally had been at the trial. As they were leaving he approached Martha briefly. 'A fine spectacle, was it not? Though perhaps not quite up to Smock Alley standards? Would you agree?'

Martha gave him a withering glance and swept by.

'What an exhausting day,' said Lady Abigail as they entered Merrion Square. 'And all for nothing.'

For once Martha giggled with Clarissa who said behind her hand, 'I really do believe she wanted the drama of a conviction. And then she would have moved heaven and earth – and Lord Clare – to have the verdict overturned.'

'Children, to your beds.'

'But I'm not in the least tired,' protested Martha.

'You will be at ten o'clock.. We don't leave for the ball until then.'

In Martha's bedroom Breege was waiting for them with a tray of cold meats. 'Eat up,' she ordered. 'You won't get another bite until two o'clock tomorrow morning.'

'Where's Matilda?' asked Martha as they settled down before the fire.

'She's gone to visit some friends of hers – the Moores in Thomas Street. There's a Miss Moore, don't know what her name is. Personally I think the great attraction is a French tutor Miss Moore has. Matilda thinks he's *trés distingué*!'

'Who exactly is Matilda? What relationship is she to the family. She eats with us but she didn't come to the trial with us. And she's not coming to the ball.'

'It's all very complicated. She is a distant relation, second cousin, twice removed or some such thing. Her parents died when she was about ten. She had no brothers or sisters; only an elderly aunt with one foot in the grave. So Mama said she should come and live with us, be a kind of companion when she gets older – by which time I'll have flown the nest. Picture Mama on long winter nights with no one to talk to, I mean, no one to listen to her! I can't see Cedric or Cecil filling that gap.'

'So she really has no one in the world. How sad.' Martha thought of her brothers, for the first time seeing them as an asset instead of a liability. She remembered Hugh particularly, and how he always took her side when her mother was fractious.

'Well, she has us. And she'll always have a home here. Even if she doesn't get married, someone will look after her. Every family has its stock of Matildas. Sometimes when one goes to family dinners it's amazing who turns up. At the Hely Hutchinsons the other night, two very old ladies descended from the attics. Mama was quite amazed, thought they had been dead for many a year.

'But to go back to Matilda – it's doubtful if she'll ever marry. No dowry. Young men just aren't interested in beautiful young ladies – if they are poor. And what lengths they go to to capture a fortune! They say of Lord Montague that he was determined to marry the Duchess of Albemarle who was rich beyond belief. But she gave out that she would only consider a sovereign prince. So he pretended that he was the Emperor of China and married her under that title. Imagine! To the day of her death she believed she was an empress and had to be served on bended knees.'

'I think the tutor is interested in Matilda,' said Martha.

'Old James Barrett? Not that he's old – it's just that one always thinks of tutors and teachers as being half as old as Methuselah. Do you really think so? Come to think of it, he always escorts her to Moores!

'That's an idea. We'll match-make, you and I. Mama could set him up in a little school like Dr Ball in Ship Street . . .' She suddenly turned to Martha and said impulsively, 'Oh, Martha, I wish I had a sister like you. It's such fun talking together.'

'So do I, Clarissa.'

'But you have Charlotte. But, of course, she's not yet ten. That isn't much use.'

'You have Matilda.'

'It's not quite the same. Matilda is a very earnest young lady, or hadn't you noticed? Always with her head stuck in a book – and such heavy books! I know I'm giddy. Charles and Andrew are always lecturing me about it. Not to mention Mama. But if one can't be giddy at the age of sixteen, when can one be? In a few years' time I'll be married, with a house to look after and children and servants. So let's be giddy while there's still time . . .'

As Martha sipped her glass of watered white wine and ate a little chicken and some strawberries, she couldn't help thinking, 'This is exactly how it should be. Happiness, love, warmth and companionship . . . and the great ball to come.

She slid in among the warmed sheets and instantly fell asleep, the menacing stomp of McNally's leg vanished from her dreams.

6   The Viceregal Ball

Awaking in the still bright evening, Martha washed herself in water scented with rose petals. Breege slipped on her underclothes and helped her to pull on pale stockings and yellow slippers.

'I'll do your hair now,' and Breege deftly wielded the ancient pair of curling irons, which every now and then she heated on the pan of hot charcoal that she had placed in the fireplace. 'I've asked Mrs Taylor to send Joseph for a new pair of tongs time and time again but he always comes back without them.'

'They're very handy,' said Martha as Breege piled her hair high at the back of her head in glossy ringlets, and fluffed short tendrils on her forehead and in front of her ears, giving the style a softer look. 'Where do you get them?'

'In Hell.'

'*Where?*'

'Oh, Miss, you wouldn't know about it. It's a shopping street near Christchurch. You get them there for eight pence.'

Now she was ready for her dress. Breege slipped it over her head, fastened the back and stood in admiration. 'Oh, Miss Martha, you will surely turn heads this night.'

As in a dream, Martha drifted down the stairs. Hearing a sound from the floor above she looked up. Cedric and Cecil were standing on the top landing. She waved to them.

Lady Abigail was waiting in the morning-room with Clarissa, who was dressed in pale blue tulle embroidered with tiny white flowers.

'You will do. Certainly you will do!' she said approvingly to Martha. 'Perfect. No need for jewellery with that wonderful young complexion.' She herself was wearing a heavy pearl choker and diamonds glittered on her arms and in her hair. 'And now I have something for you,' handing her a walnut. Martha took it, wondering uncertainly what she should do with it.

'Open it!' As Martha fumbled, Clarissa took it from her and deftly lifted off the top. Inside was a pair of very fine creamy gloves.

'There, a pair of Limerick gloves for you.' Lady Abigail

smiled. 'Every lady should have Limerick gloves. You know the test – so fine that you can pull them through a wedding ring. Though indeed I've often wondered about that. Depends on the size of the wedding ring, doesn't it?

'And now I have another present for you. Matilda specially asked that you take her fan,' flicking open a beautifully painted ivory fan. 'It belonged to her mother.'

'But I couldn't,' protested Martha, overwhelmed by all this generosity.

'Why not? There's no point in fine clothes and trinkets sitting at home. Should be at the ball. Just don't lose them! Now we'll go and show ourselves to Lord Merrion.'

Lord Merrion was in his usual wing chair in the drawing-room. He was not, it appeared, going to the ball. One of his legs was propped up on a small stool and Martha gathered that the too-tight shoes had taken their toll. A flask of what looked like brandy stood on the small table beside him.

'Splendid,' he said. ''Pon my soul. Couldn't tell her from Emily, could you?'

George and Sophie were also in the drawing-room, Sophie in white silk, with festoons of silver flowers at the hemline. She handed Martha an embroidered Kashmir shawl and as Martha demurred said laughingly, 'It's only my second-best shawl!'

Martha draped it around her shoulders, drew on her gloves, and dangling Matilda's fan by its silken cord from her wrist, she walked downstairs and through the front door.

Cinderella was going to the ball.

Even at this late hour, the streets were astir as they drove through. People were coming from the theatre, carriages and horses were waiting for their owners or trotting briskly homewards or to suppers and balls. At the corner of College Green stood a line of sedan-chairs and small carriages that Lady Abigail explained were 'noddies', which were available for hire. Hordes of beggars and urchins congregated in doorways or ran after the carriages, shouting for alms.

Martha tried to shut her eyes to the squalor and poverty of the streets and concentrate instead on the pleasure of going to her first ball. She only partially succeeded.

'I do wish it was Dublin Castle,' fretted Lady Abigail as they proceeded along the quays. 'It's so much grander. The balls are held in St Patrick's Hall and between dances people walk in the long gallery where cold meats and wines are laid out.'

'That's the nicest part,' said Sophie. 'The gallery is like a fairyland, with luminous paintings shining as if lit by moonlight, unseen figures playing and the air fragrant with lavender water. It is very very romantic.'

'A relief from the starch of the ballroom,' agreed Clarissa. 'There everyone is on their dignity, waiting to pounce if any lowly person sits or stands in the wrong place. The Viceregal Lodge dances are much more fun.'

'Now, Clarissa,' frowned Lady Abigail. 'I won't have you poking fun at rank. It's only right that peeresses and their families take precedence. These privileges must be safeguarded.' Here Clarissa gave Martha a most unladylike wink which fortunately neither of the others saw. 'I can't say I'm impressed with the Viceregal Lodge,' she continued. 'It's really only a glorified country house and not a very grand one at that. They've made a bit of an effort lately and added an extra storey to the two wings, but it's a poor residence for a Viceroy.'

'Does he not live in the Castle?' said Martha.

'No, it's held to be unhealthy. One of the under-secretaries has succumbed, turned pale as a ghost, I'm told – they call him the 'castle spectre'. At one time the Viceroy lived in Leixlip Castle – *much* more suitable.'

'Still, I suppose we must be glad we don't have to travel all that way,' said Sophie.

'I'm only sorry Martha won't have a chance of seeing Lord Camden in the robes of the Most Illustrious Order of St Patrick.'

'They're rather splendid,' agreed Clarissa. 'A silk suit and a great swirling cloak of blue velvet and the most fantastic hat, with plumes of feathers on it.'

They were now in Phoenix Park and the lights at the great gates had already been lit, though dusk was only beginning to fall on this balmy May evening. They drove along a road bordered with young trees, glimpsing in the distance dark clumps of more venerable oaks and chestnuts which gave depth and variety to the flat landscape.

'Deer, how lovely,' said Martha, seeing a herd of deer which was grazing quite close to the roadway.

'It was once the royal deerpark,' said Lady Abigail. 'Imagine all this was destined for the favourite of King Charles, Lady Castlemaine. Luckily the people of Dublin said no.'

An open carriage passed them at a fast pace. In it was seated a middle-aged man, with a heavy florid face, who looked neither to right nor to left.

Lady Abigail's lip turned down slightly at the corner. 'John Beresford. Drives everywhere in an open carriage to show his contempt for the mob. I'm not surprised that his wife makes other arrangements, so as to arrive without being blown to pieces.'

Lady Abigail had been right. The Viceregal Lodge was a rather plain house, its only point of interest being the semi-circular window over the front door and the row of urns on the parapets. Curved walls extended from the house, terminating in two two-storey wings.

Joseph stopped the carriage exactly opposite the front door and a liveried footman showed them into the hall,

where they took their place in line with the other guests who were waiting to be greeted by the Viceroy and his wife.

'That's Lord Camden,' whispered Clarissa as they edged forward, indicating a young, round-faced and rather portly man who, rather disappointingly, was not wearing his St Patrick cloak of velvet. But he did have an imposing chain which was suspended from two huge medallions on his shoulders. Lady Camden was more colourful in bright green satin.

The Merrions and the Camdens seemed to know each other well and the exchange of pleasantries was genuine and friendly. Lady Camden complimented Clarissa and Lord Camden, raising Martha from her curtsey, said, 'Charming, Lady Abigail,' adding a little pompously, 'You've been hiding a pearl of great price.'

Martha blushed and as they walked on she found Andrew at her side. Together the party went into the room to the right of the hall and found seats.

'What happens if no one dances with us,' said Martha to Clarissa.

'Don't worry! Mama always has what she calls her "gentlemen-in-waiting" standing around. If she gives the signal, one of them comes over and asks us to dance . . . Now, don't expect anything wonderful. Matilda said something very funny to me once when we had a dance at home, "God made him, therefore let him pass for a man." She really comes out with the funniest expressions.'

Lady Abigail still seemed determined to find fault with the Viceregal Lodge. 'Very ill disposed. One sits in one room, dances in another and has supper in another. One spends one's time crossing and recrossing the hall.'

Clarissa gently nudged Martha, who was quick to see that the younger people might well appreciate the freedom of movement that Lady Abigail deplored. 'You can have no idea of what a ball was like in the old days, in the

Beefeaters' Hall in Dublin Castle. The ladies sat in tiers, rising up to the ceiling. The men stood outside a railing. Every movement was noted and discussed. It must have been terrible. I must ask Grandmama about it when we go to Wexford.'

'You are going to Wexford?'

'Always in June. To Amberly. Are you not to come with us?'

'Clarissa,' she began, then stopped. This was not the time nor the place. But warn her she must. She would find some way before the night was out.

Then, as she sat back and looked around her, she had a sudden moment of doubt. Were they really to perform a simple country dance before all these great people, the cream of Dublin society, their riches and consequence conveyed in their expensive clothes? What if the whole thing was a terrible flop?

Andrew seemed to sense what was going through her mind. He bent his head towards her. 'As you said only last night to William, "All the best people seem to have been born with two left feet!" Don't let this glitter deceive you. You can dance as well as any of them. And certainly more gracefully!'

Greatly reassured, Martha relaxed sufficiently to listen to Lady Abigail and Clarissa discuss the celebrities. George had disappeared, 'Gone to the basset table,' said Sophie resignedly. 'Well, at least, they don't play for as high stakes here as they do at Daly's.'

'But I thought this was a ball.' said Martha.

'And so it is. But you don't imagine that all these old ladies and gentlemen will spend the night hopping about on the ballroom floor. One formal dance or two and most of them will go into the card-rooms.'

'Ah, Lord Castlereagh.' Lady Abigail was speaking to a tall young man whose handsome features, chiselled to

Greek perfection, seemed carved out of stone. He kissed her
hand and bowed to the rest of the party. 'Now, let us talk
for a moment about Lord . . .' here her voice dropped to a
whisper.

He made a slight grimace. 'Our friend seems to have a
whole legion on his side. I can only repeat what I said to
Lady Louisa Conolly, that it is the earnest wish of the
Government to do all it can for him. He is much loved and
if he can't be found no harm can come to him. I understand
that Lady Louisa passed the message to his wife.'

'That's some reassurance at any rate.'

'Lord Clare is of a like mind. He told a member of his
family, "For God's sake get him out of the country. The
ports will be thrown open to him and no hindrance
offered." '

This conversation was carried on in very low tones and
Martha was barely able to distinguish what they were saying. Gathering it was a confidential matter, she kept her
head turned away as if she were not listening. What was it
all about, she wondered? Who was the young man? What
had he done? Maybe it was a Lord Kingston case. Someone
had murdered someone and they didn't want another inef-
fectual trial.

'A man who will assuredly rise in the world,' said Lady
Abigail as Lord Castlereagh moved away. 'But as cold as a
dead fish . . . Now, the dancing is about to commence. Let
us go into the ballroom.'

Martha's first impression of the ballroom was of lightness
and elegance. The decoration was far more simple than at
Merrion Square, but huge mirrors around the walls and the
numerous chandeliers overhead combined to give brilliance
and sparkle to what might otherwise have been a plain
room.

The first dance, led off by Lord and Lady Camden, was a
rather formal quadrille in which the dancers, mainly

dressed in the stiff fabrics of court fashion of times gone by, bowed and curtsied to each other and performed intricate circling movements. Martha was glad she wasn't taking part, though as she watched the dancers she had to agree with Andrew. They had all obviously been very well taught but none of them radiated any sense of joy or spontaneity. She felt her confidence rising.

William had arrived and led Clarissa off for the next dance. Martha looked around for Andrew but he had gone into the hall where he was deep in conversation with some elderly gentlemen. To her annoyance George came up and said, 'Sophie has asked me to dance with you, cousin Martha.'

Her heart sank. What an irony if, on the brink of the long-awaited ball, she was about to be unmasked as an imposter. Luckily he was so busy counting quavers and concentrating on his feet that he had no energy left to talk. He was a poor dancer, and by observing the couples around her Martha managed quite creditably in what seemed to her to be an informal kind of minuet.

'I see Lord Charlemont is here,' Lady Abigail was saying when they returned to the group in the drawing-room which now included the ländler dancers.

Martha saw a large man with a rather sad face in a powdered wig with side curls, his colourful brocade waistcoat stretched across an ample abdomen. Beside him was his wife, a tiny figure in purple satin.

'I hear he has a tame mouse, and that it sits on the floor beside his chair at breakfast-time,' drawled Robert Latouche.

'I remember him at the head of the Volunteers, in College Green,' said Lady Abigail sadly. 'How time passes!'

Martha knew about the Volunteers, the explosion of popular feeling, the heady era when it seemed that Ireland might be free of England for ever and the whole nation was to come together, in which there was to be neither Catholic nor Protestant nor dissenter, but only Irishmen.

Had it all come to this? A rather portly gentleman in a powdered wig, notable for having breakfast with a tame mouse.

Two young men appeared before Martha, begging for the pleasure of a dance. Lady Abigail adjudicated and the pink-faced young man who was, he told her, in the uniform of Lord Fingall's yeomanry, led her into the dance. He was pleasant and talked of routs and ridottos, masked balls and opera, suppers and assemblies until Martha's head was spinning. Luckily he didn't seem to expect any replies, accepting her explanation that she had only just arrived in Dublin and that social life in Donegal could offer nothing on so comprehensive a scale.

But where was Andrew? Was her first ball to leave bitter-sweet memories?

In the lull after the dance, a footman announced, 'Pray silence for a special performance of the ländler by Lady Clarissa Cobbett and her friends.'

Danny, fiddle at the ready, was already standing on the small platform where the orchestra had been playing. William led Clarissa on to the dance floor. Colclough and Lady Isabella Fitzgerald, Caroline and Robert Latouche, and Andrew and Martha followed. As they took their places, the crowd, now swollen by an influx from the other rooms, pressed forward but was restrained by barriers of ribband held by a number of men.

While waiting for the music to begin, Andrew said, 'Forgive me for disappearing. I had to see to my father. His heart is weak and I think the strain of today was too much for him. But he would insist on coming . . . Besides,' he smiled, 'I can't be seen to dance *too* much with you. Look at that ring of dowagers. Even at this minute they are talk-ing about you. You are the centre of speculation. Who are

you? Where you come from? What family do you belong to?
How long do you stay among us? Lady Abigail will be
plagued with questions . . . So I must be circumspect.
However, after this, supper will be announced and Lady
Abigail promised I could partner you.'

Danny started to play. The eight young dancers bowed to
their partners and to one another and the ländler began.

Martha was in a cloud of happiness. And as they danced,
twisting and swaying to the haunting melody, the ballroom
with its glittering lights and great mirrors, the crowds and
the hubbub of conversation vanished, and she was alone
with Andrew, lost in a world of their own.

She forgot that she had promised to keep an eye on
William, that she was to give a lead to Lady Isabella, that
she was to indicate to Danny when to repeat the music. All
she could think of was how supremely happy she felt, a happiness that was so tangible that her slender graceful figure
became the focus of attention for all the onlookers.

Not indeed that she need have worried about the other
dancers. Given four handsome young men and four pretty
girls in romantic dresses, the odd mis-step, the occasional
twirl in the wrong direction, went unnoticed. Not a man
looking on but wished he were twenty again. Not a woman
saw them but sighed for the lost beauty of youth.

Then suddenly it was over. The music ceased and the
spell of the ländler was stilled. For a few seconds the dying
chords of the last bars seemed to linger in the air. Then all
was silence before the applause rang out. 'I'll remember this
night as long as I live,' thought Martha.

Lord and Lady Camden led the procession into the supper
room. He beckoned to Martha and Andrew and, with the
other dancers, they followed the Viceroy, the crowd parting
to allow a path through. It was a royal procession.

In the supper-room the centrepiece was a holly tree lit

with a hundred wax tapers. Around it, tables with white cloths reaching to the ground were laden with all kinds of dishes – chicken, meats, salads, fruits and sweetmeats, each section divided by handsome floral arrangements. Small tables, covered with white cloths and decorated with bouquets of pale-pink camillas, were placed around the walls, and servants were in attendance to help everyone to what they wanted.

When the Viceroy and his party had been served and they withdrew to a railed-off section of the room, Martha was amused at the stampede to the tables. 'Wait here,' advised Andrew. 'I'll go and forage.' He led her to one of the small tables and then returned to the fray. Martha looked around the room with lively curiosity, admiring the walls which were covered with pale-blue damask, the portraits in heavy gilt frames (presumably of past Viceroys) hung from long thick cords, the elegant sideboards and the massive mahogany wine-coolers.

Andrew returned with two plates. 'I hope I guessed right.'

'Delicious,' said Martha. She was by now very hungry and the slices of cold turkey, ham and salmon looked very welcome.

Andrew had brought her a glass of white wine and as he placed it before her, he said teasingly, 'Now I'm going to ask you to drink with me. What shall the toast be? I know what mine will be: To the girl with the violet eyes.'

As they drank to each other, silence stretched between them. Then another rush of supper seekers brought them back to earth.

'Tell me, who are the people around Lord Camden. Castlereagh I know. But who is that tall man?'

'Describe him – I can't see at the moment.'

'Low forehead, long nose, dark eyebrows, a face like a long-beaked bird of prey, with brilliant eyes.'

'Excellent! That will be John Fitzgibbon, Lord Clare. Black Jack, as he is known. One of the most powerful men in the country. Did you not hear Barrington talk about him? . . . give me another description.'

'Very slight. Spindly looking, shambling walk. Face yellow, furrowed. But when he speaks his eyes sparkle, his face lights up, his movements are quick and emphatic.'

'John Philpot Curran to the life. One of the liveliest wits in the country. A barrister at the top of his profession. When Fitzgibbon was a judge he let it be known that Curran was *unlikely* ever to win a case in his court – such was the impartiality of the law as administered in those days . . . But how marvellously you describe with a few words. I think you will shortly be writing a novel that will cause Fanny Burney to look to her laurels.'

'Curran? He has a daughter called Sarah, has he not?'

'He has . . . do you know her?'

'I've never actually met her. Is she here tonight?'

'That I don't know. I have heard that Curran dotes on one of his daughters – I'm not sure which . . . Now I'll go back and get you a dish of something by way of dessert.'

Martha studied Curran. How surprised he would be if she went up to him and told him that, in a few short years, the man beloved of his daughter Sarah would be put to death for leading yet another rising.

Andrew was back. 'Jelly and custard – the selection is a little low. I met poor old Mrs French sitting on a chair by one of the big tables – a very hazardous spot to place herself in. I helped her to an outlying chair and there she sits, fanning herself, hardly knowing whether she is alive or dead . . . The crush in here is getting unbearable; let us take a stroll in the garden.'

'Should we look for the others?'

'Impossible in this crowd. Your pretty dress would get a baptism of claret or be ripped by somebody's jewellery.'

Outside, the rustle of leaves all around them, they walked down one of the pathways bordered with boxwood. The thin crescent of the night before had grown into a quarter moon and had moved westward in the sky.

Martha, still flushed with the excitement of the night, hummed to herself and occasionally broke off into a few dance steps.

'Oh, Andrew,' she said, 'I'll never forget tonight. Never. Ever. But tell me about yourself. I'm curious. Who are you? I know you're Lord Andrew something, that you are studying law and go to dinners and balls. What else?'

'There's not much else.' Again that light bantering tone. 'I am that most despised of all things. A younger son. My brother will become Earl of Rossinver, which explains why I am slaving away at the bar instead of walking our estates in Sligo and Donegal, falling into bogholes, riding to hounds and blazing away at snipe and any neighbour who puts his head over my boundaries. It's all a little unfair. I love the country. Killoran hates it. He likes the lights of Dublin and London – he can't bear to think of being marooned in the wilds. Equally, to tell the truth, I am not looking forward to a life in crowded city streets.'

'Why can't you swap places?'

'Impossible! But Miss Martha I must confess to you. Being a younger son is not my only curse. It goes deeper, far deeper than that.'

'What can you mean?'

'Think back on the people you have met here tonight. You were introduced to Lords Camden and Castlereagh. And who caught your eye to inspire such vivid descriptions? With what letter do their names begin? You would doubtless have noted Lord Clonmell, were he here – only illness causes his absence. And we must not overlook Lord Charlemont. You will go to Carton, or to Castletown to visit the Conollys. And should you wish to take a lawsuit you are sure to engage John Philpot Curran.

'You see Miss Martha, my disability is that I answer to the wrong letter of the alphabet. Morrison! An "M"? Ah, to have been born Carnew or Crosbie. Anything that begins with a "C".'

Martha could only laugh. 'But what about John Beresford? Is he not successful?'

'Ah, but let us give him his full name – John *Claudius* Beresford. I feel he, too, must have felt the lack of a "C" and taken damage limitation action. Ponder the case of John Jeffrey Pratt. A cypher. Make him Lord Camden and he becomes Viceroy. What about Henry Luttrell? Nobody until he became Lord Carhampton. Then his daughter marries the Duke of Cumberland. No, Miss Martha, I am doomed to be a failure.'

'He stopped and took her hand, 'I jest, but there is a germ of truth in all this. I wish I could offer you something. That it was in my power to . . .' Again he stopped. 'Why do I have this strange feeling of ease when I'm with you? As if I've always known you . . .'

Martha fingered the ruby ring nervously. Should she tell him all about it, explain that this would be the last night she would ever see him? That she had meant to leave after the ländler but had lacked the resolution.

As she hesitated, a breathless Clarissa came running along the path.

'Lord Camden wants us to dance again. Do hurry. We're all waiting for you.

After the encore, again received rapturously, Martha returned to Lady Abigail's side where one of the gentlemen-in-waiting, a heavy, serious, middle-aged man introduced himself as Mr Gibbon.

'Estates in Kilkenny. Looking for a wife – his first died a year ago, leaving him with six children. A solid character.

Think of the orphans,' whispered Lady Abigail as Martha
stooped to adjust a slipper strap.

Solid – and dull. His talk was of the Duke of Ormonde
and Kilkenny Castle and the prospect of an occasional invi-
tation to a grand supper in the long gallery. Was she interested in the theatre? Martha winced and hastily said no.
Had she seen any of the products of the great Waterford
Glass Works? He had personally been friendly with old
William Penrose who died three years ago. The business
was now up for sale. The prohibition on the export of glass
from Ireland had hit all the glass-houses very badly but
since that ban was removed in 1780 they had all prospered,
Waterford being the most famous. He had a unique collec-
tion of Waterford rummers, flutes, punch jugs, goblets and
decanters that he hoped she would see one day.

'How dull he makes everything sound,' thought Martha. She couldn't help saying, 'I can see you like glass.'

'Yes,' he said complacently, 'I like glass. There is something fragile about it – as there is about a young lady.' Martha stored up this ponderous compliment to retail to Clarissa.

Having fulfilled the social side of the conversation with topics likely to interest a young lady, Mr Gibbon soon moved on to his real love and the talk centred on bullocks and bulls, calves and milch cattle until Martha could have screamed. 'He's just like an old farmer at home,' she decided. 'With a touch of country schoolmaster thrown in. As for dancing, forget it,' as he stepped on her toes for the tenth time.

Andrew claimed her again. 'I hear from Lady Abigail you've made a conquest. Six hundred acres of prime Kilkenny land. £6,000 a year. On the hoof. I feel I'm coming between you and true love.'

Martha tapped him sharply with Matilda's fan and as they twirled away, she heard somebody say, 'What a charming couple they make.'

The rest of the night passed in an enchanted haze. There always seemed to be a rush of young men waiting to ask her to dance, so Lady Abigail's coterie of gentlemen-in-waiting was released to go to the card rooms. She danced with William, who told her about the knight who spent an entire night gambling at Daly's, stumbling out in the grey of early morning having lost every acre he possessed.

Robert described the diversions of the Trinity students of his father's generation – flinging halfpences at windows and breaking them, throwing gunpowder squibs at street lamps, and large crackers into china and glass shops.

'Were they never caught?' asked Martha.

'They were too many of them. All from the very best families. How could they all be expelled or rusticated.

Besides they were cunning. They sometimes paid the watchmen to lend them cloaks so that they could disguise themselves; by way of reward they broke into gambling houses and took the stakes which they then gave to the watchmen – why, Miss Martha, you're looking horrified. Believe me, if I gave you the names of some of those unruly students you would be quite surprised at how respectably they all turned out.'

'There's nothing new under the sun,' was all Martha could say.

Colclough had a story, about Wexford. 'Members of the House always attended in full dress. One night they were debating the fate of £60,000 then lying in the Irish Treasury. Some wanted to give it to the king, some wanted it to stay in Ireland. Just as the vote was being taken the sergeant-at-arms reported that a member wanted to force his way into the house, undressed, in dirty boots and splashed up to the shoulders. It was old Tottenham, the member for New Ross, who had ridden all night, sixty miles, to give his vote for the country. They let him in. The numbers were equal and his was the casting vote. So if anyone ever toasts "Tottenham in his boots," you'll know what it's about.'

Andrew appeared again and then there was another cold collation. More dancing. And now the dawn was breaking and the sound of carriage wheels could be heard on the gravelled sweep before the front door.

The great ball was over.

In the hall, Andrew pressed Martha's hand. 'I'll be in Stephen's Green at four o'clock. And the theatre tomorrow night. I'll see you in either place.'

As they drove away, Martha was in turmoil. She had planned to make her second wish sometime during the ball (the thought of the 'gentlemen-in-waiting' had concentrated her mind). Then she had decided to wait until after the ball. Now something within her was saying, 'Let me see him once again. I'll just wait until tomorrow afternoon. It's only a few hours longer . . . I must see him one last time.'

Her mind made up, she climbed the stairs light-footedly, beating Clarissa to the third floor. She had told Breege not to get up early to be there when she came home, and as she discarded shawl, dress, underslip, stockings, slippers, all she could think of was the marvellous ball. And Andrew.

Just before she fell asleep an astounding thought crossed her mind. All the stories, all the anecdotes, had been of the present day or of a generation or two past. No one had mentioned Brian Boru, Dermot MacMurrough, the Norman invasion, the Elizabethan Rebellion. History began with King William. Or, at the very earliest, with James the First.

7 James

Martha slept late and Breege did not wake her until noon. Dressing hastily she went down to the breakfast-room where she found Matilda. There was no sign of Lady Abigail or Clarissa or Lord Merrion. The breakfast things were laid out and a servant came in with hot rolls and freshly made coffee.

'How was the ball?' asked Matilda. She seemed in low spirits. Martha wondered if she resented the fact that she had not been invited.

'It was splendid . . . but I'm sure you've been to lots of balls like it. It was a special occasion for me. My first big ball. And, Matilda, I want to thank you specially for the fan. It was much admired. I have it safely upstairs for you.'

Matilda turned a pale face towards her. Martha could see that she had been crying.

'What is it, Matilda?' She was shocked. While she had been enjoying herself, poor Matilda must have been feeling miserably rejected.

'Martha, something terrible happened yesterday. I don't know what to do.'

'Tell me,' said Martha. 'Was this when you went to see your friends, the Moores.' What was she about to tell her? That she had been attacked by foot-pads? Lady Abigail had warned that Thomas Street could be a dangerous place as it was so near the Liberties. But James had been with her, and the Moores would surely have made sure that they got home to Merrion Square safely.

The servant came back to ask if they wanted anything else. Matilda thanked him and said that they were finished. Turning to Martha she said, 'It's such a lovely day, why don't we go out into the garden?'

One huge window of the dining-room was thrown open at the bottom and they went through it and down the steps into the garden. Martha thought with a pang of the first time she had gone into the garden – the night they had been rehearsing. Then she had the ball to look forward to. Now it was all over and in a few hours she would be back home again, leaving all this behind her.

'It's safer here,' explained Matilda. 'You never know about the servants. Who is loyal and who is not?' She paused, then turned an anguished face to Martha. 'Oh Martha, can I trust you?'

'You can, Matilda. I will never reveal anything you tell me.'

'Except for James, I have no one to confide in.'

'You were talking about loyalty,' Martha gently reminded her. 'Loyalty to who?'

'The United Irishmen, of course.'

'But what have you got to do with the United Irishmen,' stammered Martha. 'I thought I heard the other night that they were a suppressed organisation.'

'James is a United Irishman . . . But let me tell you about last evening. As you know, James came with me to Moore's. The Cobbetts know that I am friendly with Miss Moore – but they don't know why. Her father is in the United Irishmen movement. My visit there yesterday had a specific purpose. We were to be part of the group that escorted Lord Edward Fitzgerald to his new hiding-place . . .'

'Lord Edward Fitzgerald?' Martha was truly amazed.

'Yes . . . as you know he had been in hiding for the last month, ever since they put the price of £1,000 on his head, ever since he escaped arrest at Oliver Bond's. That was in March. There was a meeting of the Leinster Directory and the police had information. Almost everyone there was arrested. Lord Edward was to have been at Bond's but luckily did not attend. It is said that he was warned by a kinsman of his not to go to the meeting, but James said if that was so he would surely have passed on the warning. It must have been that he had some other urgent business.

'Lord Edward has been at Moore's for some time past. He is supposed to be a French tutor for Miss Moore. But he was in danger all the time. There are so many Castle informers and the reward of £1,000 has made the situation even worse.

'By lucky chance, a carpenter named Tuite was at work in one of the apartments of Mr Cooke – he's the Under Secretary of State – at the Castle, and he heard Cooke say that the house of James Moore of Thomas Street would be

searched for arms and traitors. Tuite told Mr Moore, who was forced to flee immediately, and a new hiding-place had to be found for Lord Edward.

'Miss Moore knows the Magans who have a house on the quays at Usher's Island. Francis Magan is a new member of the Directory and readily agreed to give shelter to Lord Edward. It was only to have been for one night as Lord Edward was to have set out for the country this morning.'

'How do you know all this?' Martha couldn't help asking.

'James has contacts. He tells me . . . not everything, but enough in case I can be of help. . . . So last evening our party set out: Lord Edward's armed bodyguard and, for appearance sake, James, Miss Moore and I . . . a harmless family party setting out on an evening's stroll.

'We had just reached the edge of the Liberties when there was a challenge ahead. It was Major Sirr, the Town-Major of Dublin. Someone must have informed. There was a scuffle . . . I was clinging to James . . . Sirr was knocked down . . . Lord Edward ran down a side street . . . one of the bodyguard was captured. Miss Moore and James and I were permitted to continue our walk – I suppose they thought we were not involved in any way.'

'And where is Lord Edward now?'

'I don't know. We went back to Moore's but he didn't return there. I suppose he thought that it was no longer safe, that somebody had informed on him and that they had tracked him from there.

'Oh, Martha, what are we to do now? The United Irishmen are depending on him.'

Martha hardly knew what to believe. Was this really happening? She knew that Lord Edward did *not* lead the Rebellion but she could hardly tell Matilda that. She decided that the best course of action was to calm Matilda and try and safeguard her and James.

'Matilda, there is nothing we can do. Depend upon it,

Lord Edward is safe. You said yourself that he has plenty of loyal houses to go to. Hc has a bodyguard and lots of friends. I'm more concerned about James. Do you think they followed you back to Moore's? If they did they will suspect both of you and may have followed you here to Merrion Square. They'll hardly arrest you but what about James?'

'If they catch him, they'll torture him to get him to reveal all he knows. Beresford likes nothing better. He has a riding-school in Marlborough Street, close to Tyrone House, his uncle Lord Waterford's place, where 'tis said he flogs prisoners to death.'

'*Lord Waterford is dead, said the Sean Van Bhoct,*' murmured Martha. So that was the inspiration for that. Aloud she said, 'We must warn James immediately. There's no time to lose.'

They went back into the dining-room and up the three flights of stairs to the schoolroom. Cedric and Cecil were running around, throwing paper darts at each other.

'Where is Mr Barrett?' both Martha and Matilda said together.

'He went out. Said he'd be back shortly, but,' gleefully, 'he hasn't come back yet.'

'How long ago was that?'

It was useless. Time had no meaning for them. Then Martha had an idea.

'The clock. At the church. Did you hear it strike twelve?

'Yes, we counted.'

'Had he gone at that stage.'

'Yes, a bit before that.'

'Did you hear the clock at eleven?'

'Yes.'

'At ten?' This was like getting blood out of a stone.

'Yes.'

'So Mr Barrett left shortly after he came in, at nine?'

'Yes, he came in, told us to read our Latin and went off.'

So James had been missing for four hours. He must have decided that he had been tailed to Merrion Square and resolved to leave as soon as possible. If he had left before the boys came into the schoolroom, his absence would have been noticed. With a bit of luck, there was every chance that after that no one would have bothered to go into the schoolroom, especially on account of the ball the night before, which meant that Lady Abigail would be sleeping late.

But where had he gone?

'He has friends,' said Matilda. 'He will find a hiding-place. But I can't go to any of them. Lady Abigail would want to know where I'm going.'

'I know. We'll ask Andrew. He'll know what to do. And I'm seeing him at four o'clock . . . what about Clarissa?

Should we tell her?'

'No. I know I can trust her, but she might inadvertently say something to Lady Abigail . . . they're on the side of the government, naturally.'

As they went back into the house, a sudden thought struck Martha. 'The other night. The mystery visitor. Was that Lord Edward?'

'Yes . . . he's Clarissa's godfather. He disguised himself as a woman and came in the back way. Ramage and Lanigan, one of the footmen, are loyal to us. Lanigan would have smuggled Lord Edward up to the morning-room. Ramage then came in and told Clarissa. She and her three friends visited him – one of them, as you know, was his niece, Lady Isabella.'

'What a terrible chance to take!'

'Yes,' rather grimly. 'He thinks he has a charmed life. When he was hiding in a house along the canal he used to go for walks at night, taking a local boy with him – jumping in and out of boats moored there. And when he was staying at Murphy's in Thomas Street, he disguised himself, again as a woman, and went to see his wife, Lady Pamela, who is staying at Moira House on Usher's Island. He gave her such a fright that she miscarried and the baby was born three months before time.'

It was all beginning to make sense.

So that was what Andrew and Clarissa had been talking about that night in such hushed tones, and why she had been asked to stop anyone going into the morning-room. The half-overheard conversation between Lady Abigail and Lord Castlereagh at the ball had also been about Lord Edward. Could it be true that the Government actually wanted him to escape? Why? Because of his connections?

For a moment Martha regretted that she hadn't gone into the morning-room that night. She could have talked to Lord Edward Fitzgerald! Then she banished the thought. It was time to plan for the afternoon. Lady Abigail had mentioned that they might go to the Rotunda Gardens. She would get Clarissa to talk her into allowing the three of them to go to St Stephen's Green instead. She would confide in Andrew. He might be able to devise some scheme for getting James safely back to the north, to his home, or even abroad.

She shivered, suddenly aware of the real and terrible danger that James was in.

She would wait until after the meeting in the Green before making her second wish.

8   Stolen!

'It's a pity it's not Sunday,' said Clarissa as the carriage turned out of Merrion Square into Merrion Street. 'Everyone comes here after church, to the Beaux' Walk. It's the fashionable side of the green, much more the *mode* than the French Walk, named for the refugees, or Leeson Walk.'

Lady Abigail had made no objection to the change of plan – Martha suspected she was glad of a restful afternoon in preparation for the theatre that night.

As the carriage turned right at the top of Merrion Street, Clarissa directed, 'Take the turn into Ely Place, then we'll go round the Square and show Miss Martha the houses before we come to Beaux' Walk.'

Martha wondered uneasily what time it was; she didn't want to miss Andrew. Then she relaxed. It could only take a minute or two and surely he would wait.

'That's Ely House. The Marquess has an enormous castle away in Rathfarnham and a folly up in the Dublin mountains. Mama says he's very extravagant . . . No 4 is where John Philpot Curran lives . . . now we're in St Stephen's Green, this is Monk's Walk . . . That's the Latouche house; I believe there are some marvellous painted doors by someone whose name I've forgotten . . . and this house here belongs to the Earl of Meath: took him long enough, Mama says, to move away from that squalid Thomas Street.' Here Martha and Matilda exchanged glances .

'No 72 there belongs to the 'Sham Squire', Francis Higgins, the only buck known to wear violet gloves and have gold tassels on his boots. He married a young lady of good family by pretending he was a man of property – actually he was a waiter in a low tavern.'

'She should have known the difference.' Matilda sounded on edge.

'Anyway the poor thing died of shock. He was sent to prison, came out and made money, heavens knows how. He owns the *Freeman's Journal*.'

'A mouthpiece for the government,' said Matilda bitterly.

'What do you read?' asked Martha curiously.

'The *Dublin Evening Post* and *Magee's Weekly Packet*. John Magee exposes corruption in high places.'

'And he might as well save his breath to cool his porridge. People like Papa won't read his papers. And people like Matilda can't do a thing about the scandals he unearths. So why does he bother? . . . The smaller house here is Clanwilliam House. The one beside it was built by Mr Whaley – in an effort to dwarf Clanwilliam House. Which it does, but it's not to be admired, is it? Oddly, one of his sons married a daughter of Lord Clanwilliam – do you suppose they spent their time arguing about the architecture of both houses? Old Whaley's nickname, by the way, was Burn-Chapel Whaley.'

'Why?' asked Martha, in an effort to hurry up the story. They were going to be late.

'He hunted papists and burned down their chapels. Because his middle name was Chapell, everyone called him Burn-Chapel Whaley . . . another son is the Buck Whaley who engaged, for a wager, to walk to Jerusalem and back within twelve months. He won the wager and made a profit of £7,000, it is said – must have come in handy as he lost £10,000 at cards shortly afterwards. There's a song about it:

Buck Whaley, lacking much some cash
And being used to cut a dash,
He wagered full ten thousand pound
He'd visit soon the Holy Ground'

Instructing Joseph that they would be back within the hour the three girls strolled along Beaux' Walk. Once or twice Martha was sure that she saw Andrew, but each time it turned out to be a stranger. Her anxiety mounted. Had they missed him? She had promised to try and help Matilda but she was all the time aware that the hours were slipping by and she must decide when to make her second wish. Matilda, too, was preoccupied, looking earnestly at every passing face as if she expected that one might turn out to be James.

'In the old days, we would have seen Buck Whaley, the Sham Squire and old Copper-faced Jack Scott, Lord Clonmell – they were always together . . .' Clarissa, who was chattering away all the time, finally came to a halt. 'Here I am, talking my head off. And not a word from the pair of you. What's wrong?'

'I'm sorry,' apologised Martha. 'I was expecting to see someone.'

'Ah, Andrew.'

'Yes, he said he would be here at four o'clock.'

'Well, you can't have missed him. We weren't that much after four o'clock. He would have waited.'

But the minutes ticked by and he did not appear.

'We've missed him,' Martha said finally. 'He said he would meet me here and at the theatre tonight.'

'So why worry? He mustn't have been able to come this afternoon. Probably seeing the old gentlemen – his father – off to the country. You'll see him tonight. What's playing anyway?'

'*Robin Hood*,' said Matilda in a mechanical voice.

Clarissa shot a glance at her. 'I won't ask *you* what the matter is because I think I can guess. Mama called me in just before we came out. James has disappeared! and she thinks everyone is in some kind of plot to cover up for him. Breege because she gave the boys something to eat and Lanigan who allowed them to play in the coach house – much more to their taste than Latin or spelling. I said he'd probably gone to see a sick aunt and would be back before nightfall. He's such a sobersides. I can't imagine him disappearing without good reason, can you?'

Martha looked at Matilda. They knew the reason for his disappearance and the knowledge brought no comfort. When Clarissa turned aside to greet a friend, she squeezed Matilda's hand. 'Try not to worry. Andrew will be there tonight. He will help us.'

'I won't go tonight,' said Matilda. 'Just in case he comes back. He may need something. He must have gone off in a terrible hurry this morning.'

'Can you trust all the servants?'

'I know the ones I can. I don't trust Hallsworth. He never stops boasting about his brother in the yeomanry and how he helps to hunt down rebels. And there used to be a woman called Jenny who was always snooping around but luckily she's left.'

At supper before going to the theatre, Lady Abigail was loud in complaints about James. 'A sly one. Leaving the boys like that and not a word to anyone. Where does he expect to get another job? I certainly won't have him back and there'll be no reference.'

Martha wondered how Matilda could bear the ill-timed comments. Then, soberly, she remembered that Matilda had no choice. She had to put up with things.

'Have you got your fan,' asked Lady Abigail as they settled themselves in the carriage. 'It will be warm in the theatre tonight . . . what are we to see?'

'*Robin Hood*. By McNally.'

'That dreadful man. Haven't got over his appearance the other night yet. He must have the thickest neck in all Christendom. Well, I hope it's better than the last play I saw . . . I do miss Smock Alley since it closed.'

'I prefer Crow Street.' This from Sophie. 'They say Smock Alley was very badly managed. I believe that once, when the musicians refused to play because they hadn't been paid, the manager had to step into the orchestra box between acts and entertain the audience by playing the fiddle. This was in addition to playing *Othello*.'

'I suppose we must be grateful that the lighting is so much better these days. In the old days,' to Martha, 'the stage was lit by tallow candles stuck into tin circles hanging from the middle of the stage. Hardly the safest of devices. I used to keep my eye on the candles rather than on the

actors, waiting and watching for someone to snuff them out
when the holders overflowed. Now, with chandeliers, one
can at least look at the stage without alarm and they add so
much to the tone.'

'What a pity you missed *The True Born Irishman* last
month. Charles Macklin, who wrote it, died last year, they
say at the age of one hundred and seven.'

'I hope we are in time.' George was consulting his watch.
'There are no half-prices for latecomers here as there are in
London!'

They were in good time and the theatre was not uncomfortably crowded. As they made their way to their box,
which had a good view of the stage, Lady Abigail and
Sophie called greetings to their acquaintances, all of whom
were dressed as for a Viceregal ball. It was a glittering audience, the flashes of silver and gold embroidery and the
sparkle of jewellery creating a thousand highlights beneath
the chandeliers.

'See,' said Lady Abigail, 'we have a fine view of the
Viceregal box, over there, with the hangings. Look, Lady
Castlereagh is coming into the box next to it, with Thomas
and Louisa Pakenham. That's Miss Napier with them, she
would be a niece of the old Duchess of Leinster and Lady
Louisa Conolly, and a first cousin of Lord Edward's . . .
Now let's hope,' indicating the pit below them, 'that there
are no rowdy elements. And that the gallery refrains from
cat-calling and whistling . . . perhaps with Lord Camden
here some decorum will be maintained.' Having heard this,
Martha was no longer surprised at the two soldiers with
fixed bayonets who were standing like statues on either side
of the stage.

But where was Andrew? Lord Camden and his party
came in and took their seats. The play commenced. But
there was still no sign of Andrew.

Martha concentrated on the play, which her programme

described as 'a comic opera, based on the old legendary ballads affecting the ancient phraseology, by Leonard McNally and W Shields,' with seventeen new airs and adaptations of twelve old ones, not to mention additional songs by Signor Giordani. But why didn't Andrew come? Maybe he didn't like the theatre. That must be it! He would arrive in the interval.

Martha thought the play rather dreary, with Robin Hood cutting a poor down-at-the-mouth figure. But she was amazed at the energy with which the actors and actresses attacked their parts. Everything was wildly exaggerated and the pit and the galleries roared, booed and applauded with a ferocity that she could not have imagined.

At the interval, George, Clarissa and Sophie took a stroll at the back of the boxes, while Lady Abigail and Martha remained seated. She did not want to move in case she should miss Andrew. Lady Abigail pointed out various celebrities. Martha listened with impatience. Even when Jonah Barrington dropped in to see them she could barely muster a smile. Lady Abigail, who had just declared her intention of paying a call on Lord and Lady Camden, continued on her way and Barrington took her chair.

'I thought of something about the other night. You asked me if I were a friend of MacNally's.' Martha couldn't remember any such question but she let him continue, her eyes meanwhile roving around to see if Andrew was detained in another box.

'I've known MacNally this many a year but the way in which I met him was really very amusing. As you know he's a barrister – great quickness at cross-examination, adroitness at defence – a shrill, full, good bar voice – a great deal of middling intellect, is associate counsel of Curran. But the circuit bar would have nothing to do with him. Every summer I tried to vote him into the mess but always ineffectually. They cited his neglect of his person, his shrill voice, his frequenting low company as reasons. And his politics, defending Napper Tandy, didn't help.

'Anxious to get himself into the swim he began by challenging some of the most respectable members of the profession. But they would have none of him. So, having, as I said, some little intellect, he resolved on a plan which was to give me the retort *not* courteous in the court of King's Bench. I understand he later gave the reason, which was that I had used disparaging language towards the United Irishmen.

'I did what an honourable gentleman should. "McNally," I told him, "you shall meet me in the Park in an hour." Believe it or not, his eyes sparkled.

'We met within the hour. I asked Henry Harding as my second. As his, McNally had John Sheares, one of the Sheares brothers. He presented so coolly that I thought I had better lose no time, whereupon the poor fellow called out, "I am hit!" Luckily he was saved by his suspenders or gallows, as we used to call them, causing my second to call out, "You are the only rogue I ever knew that was saved by the gallows." '

'He soon recovered and after the precedent of being wounded by a King's Counsel, no barrister could afterwards refuse to give him satisfaction. The poor fellow often told me that my shot was his salvation.'

'Very interesting,' was all Martha could say.

Jonah Barrington leaned forward and said quizzically, 'I don't think you've heard a single word I've said. Why so preoccupied? Has anything upset you?'

'No, not really.' Martha made an effort to pull herself together. 'I was just thinking,' she said slowly, realising that she could hardly tell him just *what* she was thinking. 'Everyone talks of rebels and unrest. Will there be a rebellion?'

'To my way of thinking, it has to happen. The Govern-

ment underestimates the mood in the country. One can flog
people into submission – but what of their families and
friends? There are countless thousands of them out there.
The feeling is, "If I am to die, I may as well die with a pike
in my hand." '

'And who will win?'

'The rebels have numbers on their side and a cause that
to them is a burning one. But who will lead them? Who will
officer them? Who will discipline them? The names that one
hears do not inspire. They mean well. Is that enough to set
against battle-hardened veterans like General Lake, Sir John
Moore, Wellesley-Pole?

'Miss Martha, it will not be a contest: it will be carnage
. . . But then Irish rebels rarely choose their leaders wisely.
You have heard what an officer of James the Second said
after the Battle of the Boyne, "Change leaders and we'll
fight you again." '

'Poor Martha,' said George, who was the first of the party
to return to the box. 'Still being bored by the Battle of the
Boyne!'

Jonah laughed and left, bowing to the ladies. The Viceroy
was returning to his box, the audience was reseating itself.
But there was still no sign of Andrew.

Soon after the second act had started, Martha, whose eyes
were still less intent on the stage than on discovering
Andrew, noted some kind of activity in Lord Camden's box.
A messenger had approached and bent low to whisper in his
ear. Visibly startled, he looked anxiously at the box beside
him. Miss Napier rose to her feet in agitation. Lady
Castlereagh was speaking to her and Thomas Pakenham
seemed to be urging her to sit down again.

The pantomime was altogether lost on the general audience where pit and gallery were still cheering on Robin and
hissing at the Sheriff of Nottingham. Even Lady Abigail,

usually so conscious of everything around her, was engrossed in the spectacle on the stage. Martha suspected she was half asleep.

What could it all mean? Obviously nothing serious or Lord Camden would surely have left the theatre. Relieved, she turned her eyes to the stage once more. Andrew had not appeared, it was true. There was probably some perfectly rational explanation and on their return to Merrion Square there would be a message for her.

The performance was over at last. The Camdens left their box immediately, much to Lady Abigail's annoyance. 'I didn't get to speak to them during the interval. They always wait afterwards for a little while. Why not tonight?'

'Probably exhausted,' said Sophie. 'I know I am.'

'Take my arm, George. There will be a dreadful crush outside. I always hate it so when the whole theatre disgorges everyone at once. I hope the carriage is waiting. Sophie, take George's other arm. Clarissa and Martha, keep close behind.'

'Don't rush,' yawned George. 'We'll be out in a few minutes.'

The streets were swarming with people. Carriages and coaches were jostling for position and crowds of people seemed to be coming and going in all directions.

'It's that review of the yeomanry that took place tonight,' said George in annoyance. 'There are hardly any patrols to clear the streets and the usual Liberties mob has moved in.'

Martha did her best to hang on to Clarissa who had linked arms with Sophie, but a sudden surge of the crowd separated them. For a few terrible moments, she was completely on her own, surrounded by scarecrows of human beings who were pawing at her clothes, begging for alms, pushing her further and further away from her party. She tried to scream but in the noise and bustle her shouts were carried away.

One man, bolder than the others, seized her by the waist and grabbed at the little purse she was carrying. As he raised her arm to unloosen the cord around her wrist, the wavering light of a street lamp fell upon her hand – and upon the ruby ring. Quick as a flash he dropped the purse and pulled the ring from her finger. As his hand caught hers for an instant she saw that the middle finger was missing. Then he vanished into the crowd.

'Martha!' Charles was at her side. 'Are you all right? The carriage is here.' He pushed his way through the straggling crowd, which parted before his onslaught, and handed her into the carriage. She lay back exhausted, and to the sympathetic enquiries of Lady Abigail, Clarissa and Sophie she could only respond with floods of tears.

'My ring. My ruby ring. It's been stolen.'

'A bad business,' growled old Lord Merrion when they arrived back in the drawing-room. 'Where were the street patrols? They should have been there to clear the streets. Things have come to a pretty pass when decent people can't get safely home from the theatre.'

'I know it's been a terrible shock,' said Lady Abigail, 'but you mustn't let it upset you. The ring was very pretty and we'll try and get it back for you. But nothing is worth these floods of tears. If we can't find it, I'll give you another ring. It won't be a ruby, but an emerald. Much more valuable.'

'It's not the value,' sobbed Martha.

'I know . . . it's awful to lose something that means so much to you,' soothed Clarissa. 'Let's go to bed. We're all tired, and things always seem worse at night.'

Ramage and the footmen had cold meats laid out on trays, with fruit and wine. Martha took a bite, which felt like sawdust in her mouth, and said she could eat no more. Lady Abigail insisted on her having a glass of hot punch and clutching it she went upstairs.

Breege had the fire glowing and the room was warm and comfortable. But nothing could console her. The ring was gone. She would never get home. She was marooned for ever in this alien atmosphere. They would soon find out that she was not the real Martha. What would her future be then? An unpaid drudge like Matilda, at everyone's beck and call, patronised and half despised. How could she have been so feckless? Waiting on to try and help Matilda and that stupid James. And for a final farewell to a man who hadn't even bothered to turn up to meet her.

Alone and feeling betrayed, she cried herself to sleep.

9   A Confidence

When Martha awoke next morning the whole terrible events of the night before came flooding back. As she lay there, wondering what she should do next, it occurred to her that a strange silence had descended on the square. She could not hear the creaking wheels of the water cart or the clip-clop of horses' hooves, sounds she had got used to since her arrival. But of course, it was Sunday. And it must be very early as Breege had not yet arrived. Sunday? Church bells? It was strange that there were none but maybe they didn't ring them until later – to give the gentry a chance to sleep late.

A dull ache pervaded her whole being, an ache that had nothing to do with the loss of the ruby ring. Why was there no word from Andrew? She was unable to face the thought that he had broken his word to her. Something must have happened but what?

Breege came in with her chocolate and as she was raking out the fire she said, 'I heard about your ring. But you mustn't worry. They'll get it back for you. What did the robber look like?'

'I'm trying to think. It was all so sudden and there were so many people jostling about. He was about my height. Thin and wiry. Wild black hair. Dark eyes. And, oh,' she suddenly remembered, 'the middle finger of his right hand was missing. I saw that distinctly.'

'There, you *do* remember. Just tell Lady Abigail – she'll

offer a reward. And I'll spread the word downstairs.
Ramage and Lanigan have many friends in the Liberties.
They may be able to help. You'll get the ring back.'

'What time is it?'

'It's very early yet, Miss. Breakfast won't be till about
eleven because it's Sunday.'

Breakfast! Martha groaned inwardly at the thought of
having to face the family. The talk would be all about the
ruby ring and the well-meant sympathy would be hard to
bear. How could any of them know what the loss meant to
her?

'Sunday is an idle day,' went on Breege, 'and people do
as they choose. Lady Abigail, with George and Sophie, usually goes to the charity sermons.'

'The charity sermons?' Martha made an effort to sound
interested.

'The sermons are preached by well-known clergymen –
indeed some people complain they are more like actors than
clergymen. She prefers the Reverend Kirwan. He always has
a few ragged urchins at his side for better effect. Why, Lady
Abigail said that at the Capel Street Meeting House a couple of weeks ago, one gentleman was so moved that he
threw his watch and purse on the plate . . . They mean well,
of course, but they all know they'll be going home to a good
dinner and a warm fire.'

Martha thought of the hordes of beggers that seemed to
haunt the streets. 'Do you think charity will solve all that
dreadful poverty?'

'Not a chance,' said Breege cheerfully. 'There just aren't
enough rich people to go around.'

Martha was hardly listening. A daring plan was forming
itself in her mind. She would go and see Andrew. He would
help her to get the ring back if she explained why she needed it so badly. No doubt Lady Abigail would do her best
but she would probably think the offer of another ring

would compensate for the loss, while Ramage, for all his knowledge of the Liberties, might not have enough authority to make the thief disgorge the ring. It had to be Andrew. In spite of the fact that he hadn't turned up at the Beaux' Walk or the theatre, she felt instinctively that she could trust him. She would find out from Clarissa where he was staying and they would go and see him.

She felt almost cheerful at her decision. Anything was better than sitting round in this inert depression.

There was a knock on the door. Breege answered and returned with a letter.

'Someone left this in yesterday evening. It was taken up to the drawing-room to await your arrival home from the theatre. But evidently it wasn't given to you – Hallsworth found it on the mantelpiece there this morning.'

Martha was hardly surprised. With all the fuss about the ring no wonder Lord Merrion had overlooked giving her the letter. She took it with a shaky hand and opened it. It was from Andrew:

Saturday afternoon

Dear Miss Martha:

I have been called away unexpectedly. My father is ill and wants to return immediately to our house at Leixlip. I must accompany him. I will be able to return to Dublin on Monday or Tuesday and I will call to Merrion Square.

I am sending this in haste so that it may get to you before you set out for the theatre.

Please accept my sincere apologies for not meeting you this afternoon but I trust you now understand.

In haste,
Andrew

Martha's spirits soared. Everything was going to be all

right. She could rely on Andrew. Then, just as quickly, her
hopes were dashed to the ground. How could she get word
to him? For the first time the limitations of being a girl in
those days was brought home to her. There was no possibility of hopping on a bus or getting one of her brothers to
drive her in the family car. And she could imagine the look
on Lady Abigail's face if she made a request for the carriage
to make a journey down the country to see a young man she
had met twice before! That was clearly impossible. She'd
have to think of something else.

Clarissa came bounding in. 'So you're up. I couldn't
sleep either!' She gave Martha a quick hug. 'Now, you
mustn't worry about your ring. If we can't get it back,
Mama has promised you another. When you get back home
you can just say you swopped it for a better one. Take it
from me, your father will hardly know anyway. Unless,' she
suddenly looked worried, 'it was a family heirloom of
course.'

Perhaps it was the mention of home but Martha felt a
wave of homesickness sweep over her. Would she really
never see them again? How dear they all seemed now that
they were so far away.

'Oh, Clarissa,' she said in tears. 'It's much much worse
than you think. You see, it isn't an ordinary ring. It's a
magic ring . . . I made a wish and it brought me here.'

'Martha, you're so upset that you can't think straight.
The Montgomery's coach brought you here. You were staying with them in Kells, on your way from Donegal.'

'Clarissa,' Martha took a deep breath. 'I'm not Martha
Hamilton. I'm Martha McGinley. Do believe me. In any
case, you'll find out soon enough. There's bound to be a
message from the real Martha Hamilton any day now – I
can't think why it hasn't arrived before now. I only meant to
say until after the ball on Friday night . . .'

Then it all came pouring out. The dance in the school

hall. The beautiful night. The wish to go to a grand ball. Making the wish. Finding herself in Merrion Square and discovering she was back in 1798. To her amazement, Clarissa didn't question any of it. Her eyes grew rounder by the minute, and when Martha had finished speaking she said, 'What a perfectly wonderful adventure. I wish it had happened to me. Imagine being able to wish for anything you wanted in the whole wide world.'

'Then you believe me?'

'I must confess, Martha, I did wonder about you. I thought there was something that was not quite *comme il faut.* I said to Matilda how strange it was that you never talked about your family.'

'How could I? I knew hardly anything about them.'

'And you came here with a trunk of out-of-date clothes. Yet you showed us a new dance, to music no one had ever heard before.'

'It's by Schubert – he was born a year ago!' They both laughed. 'So now you see why I must get the ring back. I must get home.'

'And so you shall. What should we do? No point asking George. He's great on advice. Useless when it means action.'

'I thought of Andrew. He's had to go to Leixlip unexpectedly, that was why he didn't come to Stephen's Green or to the theatre yesterday.'

'Of course! Andrew is just the person. He knows lots of people. He'll be able to make enquiries. Ramage and Lanigan will help him.'

'But he's in Leixlip. He won't be back until tomorrow. Maybe even Tuesday. And tomorrow may be too late. The thief may have sold the ring by then and we won't be able to trace it.'

'So you want to go to Leixlip.'

'We must. It's my only chance.'

'Wait . . . I have a splendid idea. Lady Isabella Fitzgerald is going down to Lucan today, this morning. She was to have gone yesterday but she decided at the last minute to go to Lady Mountjoy's. We'll travel with her. Leixlip is only a few miles away from Lucan.'

'How can we? Your parents will wonder where we are? What will you tell them?'

'Nothing at all! Until it's too late. Mama and Papa *would* let us go if we asked. But we would have to arrange about the carriage and it would all take so long. And we'd have to listen to Papa saying there would be United Irishmen behind every bush and Mama calming him . . . no, Andrew would be back before we got there! I'll leave a note and say Lady Isabella asked us to accompany her to Lucan. After all, she'll have a coachman and two footmen with her so we'll be well guarded.'

'What about the people in Lucan? Will they mind us going there? We may not be able to get back tonight.'

'Lady Vesey will be delighted to see us. When I met her at the ball she asked if I was ever going to visit . . . Now, we haven't a moment to lose. First thing is to send Lanigan around to Leinster House to ask Lady Isabella to wait for us. Breege can take the message to him. Then get her to find the smallest trunk she can and pack up our night things and a change of gown. She can smuggle it down the back stairs to Lanigan. Then we'll go down the same way.'

'Is it safe to tell so many people?'

'We've no choice. We can do nothing by ourselves. But there's no risk. The servants won't tell on us. We're not eloping after all. Or planning to hold up a coach. It's a perfectly respectable visit with a duke's daughter.'

'What about Matilda?'

'Leave her alone. She's too worried about James. Bad enough for Mama to suspect she knew James was going and said nothing. She would be doubly furious if she learned that Matilda knew we were rushing around the countryside in pursuit of an eligible young man and didn't tell her!'

'Poor Matilda. There's no news of James then?'

'I haven't heard. I'm sure she would have told us if there was . . . now, I must rush off and write this note. This is going to be fun!'

When Breege came back after sending Lanigan to Leinster House, she looked visibly shaken.

'What's wrong, Breege?'

'Lord Edward. He was caught last night.'

'Where? When?' Martha suddenly thought of the goings and comings between the boxes in the theatre last night, the whispered conversations. Lord Camden had stayed in his box but Lady Castlereagh and Miss Napier had left.

'Are you sure you're not confusing it with the night before when Lord Edward was nearly captured?'

'I don't know, Miss. All I know that Lanigan said he had been taken.'

Martha's spirits sank. If Clarissa heard about it she might want to stay on in Dublin. What about Lady Isabella? She must have heard by now. Surely that would alter her plans? Just when everything seemed to be going right, was it all to be upset again?

'Breege,' she said urgently. 'Don't breathe a word of this to Clarissa. If it's not true, telling her would serve no purpose. It could be just a rumour. We'll be back tomorrow and everything should be clearer then.'

Breege said nothing but seemed in sombre mood as she packed the clothes.

Clarissa came in, letter in hand. 'What do you think of this?'

> Dearest Mama:
>
> In all the fuss last night I forgot to mention that Lady Isabella had asked me to accompany her to Lucan this morning. She will be leaving early so, as I didn't want to wake you, I'm leaving this note instead. We will be back tomorrow . . . You did want Martha to see Lucan House and this seemed an excellent opportunity . . . Tell Papa not to worry. We will have a stout coachman – and he is stout – and two footmen with pistols to guard us. We hope to see Andrew there and we will have his additional protection on the way back tomorrow.'
>
> > Love,
> > Clarissa

In spite of all her troubles, Martha had to laugh as she thought of Lady Abigail's reaction to such an airy letter.

'Are you going to leave it in the hall?'

'No – we'll give it to Lanigan to take back from Leinster House. The family won't be down for ages yet and we'll tell him not to give it to Mama until breakfast is almost over, unless our absence is questioned.'

As they went down the back stairs, Martha thought how quickly and expertly Clarissa had managed everything. Now all she could hope for was that news of Lord Edward's arrest, if it were true, had not reached Lady Isabella and caused any change in her plans.

10   Lucan House

As the girls, accompanied by Lanigan, walked across to Leinster House, Clarissa was chatting away gaily.

'It's rather plain on this side, isn't it? The front is much handsomer, with columns and colonnades. But it only looks out on a courtyard, while this side has lawns and there is a very pretty walk under the trees.'

'When was it built?'

'Ages ago, must be at least half a century. When Lord Kildare wanted a suitably magnificent house, the architect insisted on a site of "unlimited dimensions". So he settled on Molesworth Field which was really out in the country. For years it stood alone in its glory as Merrion Square hadn't even been thought of then. First it was Kildare House. Then he was made Duke of Leinster so it became Leinster House.'

They went in by a side door and passed, through a lofty hall with columns and an ornate stucco ceiling, into the family private apartments. Lady Isabella welcomed them and introduced them to her old nurse who was busy giving her messages to pass on to the rest of the family. To Martha's relief she did not seem to have heard the news of Lord Edward's arrest.

'Cousin Sarah was to come over last night but didn't. I suppose she decided that as I was not to be here she stayed with Lady Castlereagh instead . . . now, I think we are ready. The carriage is waiting.'

'What a pity Martha can't see over the house,' said Clarissa impulsively.

Martha had a sudden moment of panic. A tour around such a vast house would take an age and there was the possibility that a messenger would shortly arrive to announce the news of the arrest and that the journey would be deferred.

'She will, when I come back.' promised Isabella.

Clarissa was in high good humour as they jogged along, still talking of the glories of Leinster House.

'We had a marvellous ball there last summer, in the supper room which runs the whole length of the house and looks out on the lawns. Isabella showed me the view from the roof. You can see the ships in Dublin Bay and the whole coast from Howth to the Wicklow Sugar Loaves.'

Isabella smiled. 'We went up by the secret staircase.'

'A secret staircase?" said Martha.

'No one knows just why it was built. But it is so contrived as to baffle the most diligent search.'

As they turned into College Green, Clarissa said, 'How many people are about! Most unusual for early Sunday morning. And I've never seen so many soldiers . . . really, you'd think we were at war. Mama says that Camden is always being overruled by Beresford who wants the military to take over.'

Then, realising that this might be a reminder to Isabella of Lord Edward and his fugitive state, she hastily changed the subject.

But soon the sights and smells of the city were left behind as they drove through Phoenix Park and took the winding road to Chapelizod. It was a warm and sunny day, with clouds floating by in a high blue sky, and in spite of her worries Martha felt her spirits rising. The road turned and twisted with the course of the River Liffey which was sometimes visible, sometimes hidden by clumps of trees that grew down to the water's edge, and as they slowed down to turn a corner, the murmur of the river darting over cataracts could be heard. Wild flowers sprang from the lush green grasses in the hedges on either side. The birds were singing and everything seemed to breathe of peace and contentment.

Isabella spoke little and Martha was too busy wondering what she would say to Andrew when they met to have much conversation, but Clarissa talked enough for three.

'We must be near Luttrellstown by now,' she said after they had been on the road for some time. 'Thank goodness, it's such a beautiful day. I'd hate to be passing it at night.'

'Why ever?'

'They were a monstrous family. One of them fought with James at the Battle of the Boyne and was charged with high treason for his pains, so he fled abroad. Then they decided they would drop the charge – provided he returned to Ireland within eight months. But through his brother's treachery he never got back. So Henry got the estate! An evil man, it was said, who had an evil son and an evil grandson.

'But isn't it strange? He prospered exceedingly. Married an heiress. Got a title – Carhampton. One of his daughters married the Duke of Cumberland. 'Twas said he was completely captivated by the way she danced the minuet. It's a pity we can't see the house from the road. It's *very* splendid. Festooned with turrets. I believe they held wild gambling parties there. Killed each other in duels. Buried the bodies. One of the Luttrells was murdered, another died in debt. I think they're all gone now and nobody lives there. They say the place is haunted. The country folk around tell tales of satanic revels held by night, the house all lit up, and inside demoniac gamblers gathered around the card-table, staking the souls of men . . .'

Isabella was looking distinctly frightened when suddenly there was shouting and the carriage was jerked to a standstill. Looking out Martha could see two men in red uniforms, with white cross-banding over their shoulders and tall hats with short plumes. One was pulling at the horses' heads, the other was grappling with a footman who had leaped down from the back of the carriage. The second footman was standing, pistol cocked, trying to intervene in the struggle.

Then the man who had stopped the horses, rushed around to the carriage door and pulled it open. As he lurched forward the smell of drink was overpowering.

'Easy, ladies. We're searching you. Any green garters?'

Clarissa coolly picked up her parasol and poked him in the eye. With a scream of pain and caught off balance he fell back into the ditch. The footmen meanwhile had overpowered the other assailant and thrown him down the slope on the river side, discharging a shot after him. Then they climbed back on the carriage, the coachman cracked his whip and the horses plunged forward.

Martha realised that she had hardly had time to feel afraid before the whole incident was over. Isabella sank back with a sigh of relief, and Clarissa said with a gleam in her eye, 'I don't think we'll tell Mama about that.'

'Who were they?' asked Martha.

'Rabble in the guise of Government soldiers,' said Clarissa contemptuously. 'Probably stragglers from some regiment that's scouring the countryside for arms. In the intervals of torturing the peasantry they take time off to rob coaches and molest females. The scum of the earth.'

At Lucan they turned across the bridge over the Liffey, glimpsing Lucan House through the trees, and shortly afterwards the carriage drew up before the front door. They were shown into a large hall with yellow marble pillars and

Emily Vesey came out to greet them.

'Isabella, I hope you're not too fatigued . . . Clarissa, how pretty you looked the other night . . . And so this is Martha . . . but are you only come for such a short time? Dinner will soon be served. In the meanwhile, you might like a turn about the park. It is so pleasant in this weather.'

'But first, Mrs Vesey,' said Clarissa, 'we must beg a big favour of you.'

'Anything you want – if it's within my power.'

'A dear friend of ours, Andrew Morrison, is presently at Leixlip. We would love to see him. Can we get a message to him?'

'Ah,' Mrs Vesey's eyes twinkled. 'Does this explain the sudden very short visit? The Colonel was quite alarmed to hear you think of travelling at this time.'

Martha blushed but Clarissa said airily, 'You must think nothing of it.'

'You can rely on me! I'll get the Colonel to send Roger.'

After being cooped up in the carriage since they left Dublin, it was refreshing to stroll through the wooded estate.

'You saw the bridge which spans the river? My husband hates me to tell this story but as he isn't here I can! This is the famous bridge that his ancestor was supposed to erect at his own expense but somehow he managed to wriggle out of paying for it. Dean Swift wrote a mortifying verse:

> *Agmondisham Vesey, out of his bounty,*
> *Built a fine bridge – at the expense of the county.*

Lucan is quite famous too, for its Spa. It's on the demense here and people come from Dublin to take the waters. There's a ballroom and a curious genius called Maturin often comes down to play his fiddle for the dancing. But lately, of course, there hasn't been much activity. People don't want to travel from the city.'

As they returned to the house, a carriage was just drawing up.

Mrs Vesey looked puzzled. 'It can hardly be Roger back so soon. Why, it looks like Andrew Morrison.' She quickened her pace and went forward to greet the arrivals.

Andrew – yes, it was Andrew – was handing a lady out of the carriage.

'Lady Louisa!' said Mrs Vesey. 'You are most welcome.'

'It's Lady Louisa Conolly,' Clarissa said to Martha. 'She's a sister of Emily, the old Duchess of Leinster, lives over at Castletown House. How strange that Emily Vesey never told us she was expected.'

Isabella flew over to the great-aunt who kissed her sadly.

'Child,' she said, 'I have the most tragic news for you. Eddy is at Newgate. Under arrest.'

To Martha's surprise, Andrew had not come up to greet her when the two parties had met before the house. Merely made her a formal bow and turned away to escort Lady Louisa inside.

Was he upset about Lord Edward? But even if he were, surely there was no need to be so cold and distant. In the drawing-room he avoided her and at dinner took a seat at the far end of the table.

'What's wrong with Andrew?' whispered Clarissa.

'I have no idea.'

'Lovers' quarrel?'

'Don't be absurd.'

It was a sombre meal, the talk naturally being about Lord Edward.

'My daughter Emily and my niece, Sarah Napier, were at the theatre last night – they were in a box with Lady Castlereagh and the Pakenhams – when news was brought to Lord Camden of Edward's arrest. Of course they heard everything and Sarah was so upset that Lady Castlereagh took her out. They went straight to Moira House, knowing Lady Edward to be there. But they were told that she was not be be advised that night. So, in fact, she didn't learn the news until this morning. Sarah Napier has not left her side since.'

'But how was he apprehended?' Andrew's voice was puzzled. 'I gather he escaped capture the night before. Was he betrayed twice?'

'That we'll probably never know. I can only put together the bits and pieces I've been told from various sources . . .

'After his lucky escape when on his way to Magan's, he went back to Thomas Street where he lodged with Murphy, a feather merchant. I understand he had a cold and lay in bed all morning. There was an alarm when a party of soldiers led by Major Sirr came to Thomas Street to search Moore's house, where Eddy had lately lodged, and he had to hide in the attic.

'Nothing was found and the soldiers went away. That lunatic, Neilsen, called twice, never bothering to take precautions – but urging Eddy to be careful!'

'At seven o'clock, Murphy went upstairs to see Eddy. The police chief Swan and a young officer called Ryan followed him to the room. Eddy stabbed Swan three times but he escaped and ran down to get Major Sirr and his eight soldiers. Eddy then stabbed Ryan, whose wounds, by the way, are said to be serious. Sirr fired and Eddy was wounded in the right shoulder.

'He was overpowered and taken to the Castle by sedan chair. I believe Camden had ordered an apartment for him there but because he had wounded an officer he had to be taken to Newgate.'

'Poor Pamela,' said Mrs Vesey. 'How did she take the news?'

'Admirably, as far as I can discover . . . she says there is no evidence against him?'

'Evidence?'

'He will be tried for high treason. I understand that Lord Clare says he'll make his exit on the scaffold.'

'His wound . . . is it serious?'

'Not as far as we know . . . I have spent the day gathering all this information and writing to sister Emily about the tragedy. As no packet went today, tomorrow is the first day I can get the news away.'

'How distressing this must be to all the family,' said Colonel Vesey, but Martha, who was beside him, heard him mutter to his wife, 'Maybe some good will come of it. If what they say is true, that he was at the head of things, maybe now his arrest means the country can be at peace.'

'If they really think there is to be no further trouble ahead, why have you been ordered back to Dublin?'

'Purely a precaution, m'dear.'

Louisa was talking to Isabella. 'We would have got a message to you at Leinster House, only we thought you were gone to Carton. But, my dear, you must not dream of going there now. Ever since martial law was declared, things have gone from bad to worse. When Abercrombie was in Kildare over a month ago he issued a warning that unless arms were returned within ten days he would send the army in to live at free quarters. So for the past month Colonel Campbell and the 9th Dragoons have been let loose, to plunder, flog and burn the houses of those suspected of having arms.'

'Terrible,' said the Colonel. 'But necessary, Lady Louisa, in these times. Rebels have to be rooted out.'

'And not only rebels,' said Lady Louisa sarcastically. 'Can you imagine those rapacious soldiers quartering themselves in wretched mud hovels. No, indeed, they have taken particular care to quarter themselves in the better houses.'

'Only if they have grounds for suspicion.'

'Nothing could be easier to arrange . . . why they sent in a party to Thomas Reynolds of Kilkea Castle . . . on the grounds that Lord Edward was hiding there. Tore up the floors, hacked down the stairs, carved their names on the such furniture as they couldn't break up, smashed every piece of glass, and stole or used for target practice the paintings – many of them given to Reynolds' grandfather by his namesake, Sir Joshua. The place was a complete shell when they left.'

'What of Carton?' Lady Isabella was visibly alarmed. 'My sisters said nothing of this.'

'I do not think they were aware of all that was happening. Luckily Carton was spared, even though the Scots Fusiliers were sent there for a few days. Can you imagine! Strutting around the place, arms piled in the colonnades. Elizabeth had to write to Castlereagh to have them removed. Not much damage done fortunately, though Stoyte took the precaution of bricking up the family plate in a wall near the duke's room. Of course, the Leinsters came in for particular attention, all out of spite, not only because of his brother but because he resigned from the militia last year in protest at government methods.'

'My poor father,' said Isabella. 'What a burden this is for him, with my mother so ill.'

'How is she?' asked Emily Vesey.

'As you know he lately brought her to London but there is no definite news yet.'

'Your sisters will be on their way to Dublin tomorrow,' said Lady Louisa, 'and you must return there with Martha and Clarissa. The country is too dangerous.'

After the ladies had retired from the dining-room, Martha sent a message by the butler to ask Andrew to come and see her. In the small ante-room beside the dining-room, she awaited him. He came in, his manner still cold and formal.

'You asked to see me.'

'I must talk to you. There is a serious problem. But what is wrong? Why are you behaving so strangely . . .'

'Martha,' he burst out. 'Who are you? On our way down yesterday we stopped at an inn in Chapelizold. There, by a strange chance, I met Francis Montgomery. We were talking about the unsettled state of the country, on foot of which he told me that Martha Hamilton had decided not to go to Dublin but to return to Donegal. Due to the rumours that some coup was to be attempted in Dublin, the family did not send a message to Abigail immediately. Which he now begged me to do . . . Martha, you are not Martha Hamilton. You are an imposter . . .'

11   The Secret

'You're quite right, Andrew. I *am* an imposter. But I never meant to deceive anyone. It just happened.'

'How? You arrived and let everyone assume you were Martha Hamilton. Why?'

'I'll tell you what happened and you can tell me what you would have done . . . so sit down. You're making me nervous.'

Suddenly she knew it was going to be all right. He had come to see her. He wanted an explanation – which was reasonable enough – but he *would* believe her. He would help her.

'You remember that I told you my ruby ring was very special?'

'Yes. It was a very pretty ring but I didn't quite know what you meant by "special". I thought perhaps it was given to you by someone who loved you.'

'It was given to me by my grandmother. It's not an ordinary ring. It has power to grant two wishes . . . now, don't dismiss this as preposterous. Listen . . .'

She told him the whole story, just as she had told it to Clarissa. At the end it was quite plain that he didn't know whether to believe her or not.

'It's such a strange story. I don't know what to think.'

'Don't think at all! Just help me. If I get the ring back I can prove that it is magic. I don't ask you to believe me on my story alone. I'll prove it.'

'We'll settle on that. I'll do all I can.'

Martha held out her hand. 'Shake on it.' Seeing his star-tled look, she laughed. 'It's a custom of our time. It means we've struck a bargain. Farmers do it at fairs . . . indeed, I'm sure they do it down the country but maybe not in Merrion Square or Lucan House . . . Incidentally, I think we should have Clarissa in. She may have some ideas.'

'Clarissa? She's a feather-brain.'

'Actually she's not. You should have seen her today, pok-ing that soldier in the eye . . . oh, I forgot. I was to say noth-ing about it.'

She told him what had happened and he was horrified.

'It was most reckless of you all to come down. You heard what Louisa said. This part of the country is aflame. Because of Lord Edward they seem to think everyone in these parts is a rebel, and the more arms they find, the more ruthless the searches. . . . Now we had better plan how to get the ring back, as we won't have time to think of any-thing tomorrow except getting safely back to Dublin.'

As Martha described the thief again, Clarissa broke in, 'Did he say anything? Did you hear him speak?'

'No, he just grabbed the ring.'

'Pity . . . Dublin is said to be full of well-dressed people with English accents, all of them robbers.'

'Well, he certainly wasn't well-dressed.'

'Let's rule out England then. Maybe he was up from the country.'

'Most of the beggers in Dublin are. They come here when the turf-cutting is over and the harvest hasn't begun,' explained Andrew. 'But it's a bit early for turf yet, isn't it? In our part of the country it's well into summer before the turf is brought home.' Martha smiled at the expression. So 'bringing home the turf' descended from times past.

'You'd know if he was from the country anyway,' said

Clarissa impishly. 'Straw in his hair . . . and very likely twice the size of the Dublin rabble . . .'

Andrew frowned. 'Clarissa, this is serious . . . Martha, was he with anyone? Some of them work in packs, especially those who hold up coaches. He didn't have a pistol . . . no? I think we can assume he was a beggar from the Liberties who wanted your money at first, then saw his chance of getting something much more valuable.'

'What will he do with the ring?'

'Sell it or pawn it. He'd probably find it difficult to sell – who'd buy a jewel from a beggar in rags? More likely he'll pawn it. Probably at a shop in the Liberties.'

'Andrew, do you really think we have a chance of getting it back?'

'But of course!' Andrew was reassurance itself. He didn't want to depress her by pointing out that the ring might already have been sold that night for a few coins to buy drink and that the trail could already be cold. Or that the pawnshops would be open tomorrow and the ring might be pawned before they got back to Dublin.

'Lots of beggars come to the back gate for food,' said Clarissa. 'Lanigan could surely find out if they know of anyone with a missing finger.'

Lady Vesey popped her head around the door.

'I don't know what plots you are hatching in here,' she said. 'But do come in and have some tea.'

There was an easier atmosphere as they sat around taking tea. Andrew was smiling, Martha happy and Lady Louisa more cheerful, as if she were accepting the view that there was no evidence against Lord Edward which would justify a charge of high treason.

'You must be wondering how we, the Veseys, came to be living at Lucan House,' said the Colonel to Martha. 'Lucan, as you know, was the title of Patrick Sarsfield. The Sarsfields were an old Catholic family and lost their lands after the Rebellion of 1641. However they got them back under Charles the Second, but as Patrick had no heirs the title died with him and the property devolved on his niece Charlotte who married my uncle Agmondisham . . .'

'My dear,' Lady Vesey broke in, 'you're boring the poor girl with all this family history.'

'Yes, indeed,' whispered Andrew to Martha. 'It must be as remote to you as the decline and fall of the Roman Empire.'

'Strangely, it isn't. I might be listening to my grandfather and a neighbour talking about who owned what land and how they got an extra few acres by making a good marriage with the only daughter of a neighbour. Nothing changes.'

Later that evening they went for a stroll in the park. The moon was about three-quarters full, its light illuminating trees, shrubs and grasses as clearly as if it were day.

'Why so serious?' asked Martha as she and Andrew dropped slightly behind the rest of the party. 'Do you really believe my story? Or are you just being polite.'

'I haven't quite made up my mind. "There are more things in Heaven and earth than are dreamed of in your philosophy, Horatio . . ." Do they still read Shakespeare?'

'They do indeed.'

'I was thinking of something else. If you do come from another age you know what happened . . . Don't tell me; I'll tell you. The Rebellion *did* happen, probably outside Dublin. It was put down savagely. Very shortly, over all our protests, Clare, and Beresford engineered the Act of Union with England. Ireland ceased to be a country . . ."

'But how do you know all this?'

'Martha, everyone knows that the British Government, with the help of the puppets in Dublin Castle, wants to sweep away Ireland and make it part of the United Kingdom, as happened with Scotland. As for the Rebellion, what chance have even thousands of men, with precious few guns and pistols, against an army with trained military commanders? How could it succeed?

'But the French are to come, you may say. The French! They always come too little and too late. Or send a fleet at the wrong time – as they did at Bantry. I have no great opinion of Napoleon. Was it Tallyrand who said of him when he returned from Africa, having lost his entire army, "Is the fellow back for another army?" '

Martha hardly knew what to say. He smiled at her. 'Well, am I right?"

'You are right.'

'I don't want to hear more . . . except, yes, one thing . . . Lord Edward. Did they charge him with high treason?'

'No.'

'That's something . . . Why not?'

'He died from his wound.'

'Perhaps it was all for the best. Poor fellow. The most high-minded man I ever knew.'

The path they were following led to the Sarsfield monument where the rest of the party was gathered.

'How beautiful,' said Martha, looking at the tall pedestal with its sculptured medallions of classical figures surmounted by an ornate funeral urn.

'I like the tortoises,' said Clarissa touching one of the heads of the three animals, the backs of which supported the monument. 'They say that Sarsfield's ghost lingers among the trees at twilight. Have you ever seen him?'

'I'm afraid it's only a pretty story,' laughed Mrs Vesey. 'Actually, he never lived here . . . Now we must return. We all have an early start tomorrow.'

As they went indoors, Martha turned for one last look at the park. Away to the west, a glow lit up the sky, an uneven glow as if something was spurting and subsiding, throwing out tongues of red, as if a fire were raging.

As she went in she thought of the irony of the situation. She knew what about to happen – that the rebellion would shortly break out. But her knowledge of the future did not extend to her own affairs. She did not know whether she would ever get home again.

Just before she fell asleep, it occurred to her, sadly, that she had forgotten to mention James to Andrew.

12 *The Rising Tide*

There was a muted and hurried farewell next morning after a hasty breakfast. 'We've no time to lose,' said the Colonel. 'If the army was at Kilcock yesterday, moving on Celbridge today, the road will shortly be impossible.'

The Veseys, too, were Dublin bound, Emily explaining that the Colonel had been ordered to report to the Dublin militia.

Martha shivered. It was really serious.

Progress was slow, as carriages, landaus, postchaises, and even great clumsy old coaches that could hardly lumber along were on the road. Men on horseback passed them by frequently. Occasionally they passed the ruins of a burnt-out cabin, the charred remains still smoking, the acrid smell filling the air.

'I wish we were riding,' said Clarissa. 'We'd be in Dublin by now. This is most provoking,' as the carriage came almost to a standstill.

'There must be blockages ahead,' said Andrew. He sounded irritable and they all found the slow pace exasperating.

Near Palmerstown, the carriage was halted by a military officer. Andrew gave his name and those of the girls, Lady Isabella being introduced as 'Lady Isabella Vesey of Lucan House.'

The captain, who seemed a pleasant young man, said,

'My apologies for this interruption. Our information is that we may be attacked by the rebels at any moment. My men are searching the countryside for arms.'

'Did you get many?'

'So far about two hundred and fifty muskets and blunderbusses, and above three hundred pike heads, all of which had been hidden in the gardens.'

He paused when the pistols of the footmen were discovered.

'I was told to take all arms.'

'And leave us without any protection?'

The captain hesitated. 'We have instructions to protect people of good character . . . so, perhaps, it will be safe to leave them with you. But watch out. The only way the rebels can get weapons is by stealing them.'

'We will not give them up,' said Andrew grimly. 'You can depend upon that . . . I understand that the main part of Colonel Campbell's army is now at Celbridge.'

'So we believe.' The young face looked worried.

'You're not from these parts,' said Andrew.

'No . . . I'm with the Wicklow militia.'

'Ah, then you must know my friend, Thomas Carnew.'

'I do indeed.'

Martha wondered why he was bothering with such pleasantries until she reflected that in a time of martial law, the military had to be assuaged.

A new fire must have just been started, for a strong smell of smoke suddenly drifted in through the carriage window. By craning her neck Martha could see that a cabin a little further up the road was in flames. Then she heard the screams. A man was tied to a wooden triangle at the side of the cabin, his tattered shirt torn off and a huge soldier began to flog him with a knotted whip. His wife and children were on their knees nearby, screaming and sobbing.

'Can't you stop it?' asked Andrew.

The captain looked unhappy. 'He's a blacksmith. He knows where the pikes are buried. The orders are to flog them until they confess.'

'And if he doesn't have any arms or know where any are hidden?'

'They'll cut him down eventually.'

'When he's dead? I believe that in Athy one man got five hundred lashes.'

'Can't you do anything?' begged Martha as the screams continued.

'Cut him down, Captain,' Andrew appealed. 'Let them search for the weapons but is torture part of your brief?'

'Cooke from the Castle said that a little military roughness was necessary,' said the Captain grimly. 'I have my orders . . . Our instructions are to treat the country as enemy territory. To burn and destroy cabins if anything gives rise to suspicion.'

Nevertheless he went up to the soldier who was flogging the blacksmith and gave an instruction. The man was cut down and his shrieking family rushed to him, and began to cover his raw and bleeding back.

'Drive on,' ordered Andrew and the horses trotted forward.

'What a relief,' said Clarissa. 'At least one poor man has been saved.'

Andrew didn't reply. His eyes met Martha's. What was to prevent the soldiers from stringing the man up again when the carriage was out of earshot. They would flog him until they got information from him. If he had pikes they would discover them. If he had none he would have to inform on neighbours. Or be flogged to death.

A grim reminder of the reality of the situation confronted them again when they turned across the bridge at Chapelizod. A man was dangling from a tree, his body festooned with green ribands.

'Why green?' Martha tried to shut out the picture of the figure hanging from the trees but could not.

'The colour of revolution. The green bough.'

'A wretched business on all sides,' said Andrew as they finally reached the quays. 'Peasants goaded into rebellion. Soldiers, the half of them foreigners, not knowing or caring why they're here. As for the blacksmith . . . if he survives today, I suspect he'll redouble his pike making.'

'Meanwhile, let's all agree on our story. Unrest in the country but we witnessed little of it. Rumours, it is true, but just rumours. Lady Abigail will accept that.'

'Splendid!' said Clarissa. 'I'm glad we have you on our side – to lend respectability to our escapade.'

Martha couldn't help laughing.

Oh, what a tangled web we weave,
When first we practise to deceive.

The reception at Merrion Square was one of relief and censure.

'How could you?' moaned Lady Abigail. 'When we got your note we were wretched. It's all very well for Isabella to take matters into her own hands, with her parents being away. But how could you have involved Martha? If anything had happened to her, how could we ever have explained it to her father.' Here Martha and Andrew exchanged glances. 'And George came in and sat for half an hour recalling all the atrocities that had happened down in the country that I'd quite forgotten.'

Clarissa threw her arms about her mother's neck and said in her usual scatter-brained way, 'Now, Mama, do forgive me. It was all my fault. I persuaded Martha and really if she hadn't come I would have been all alone coming back since Isabella was to stay at Lucan until she went to Carton.'

'And how stands the country,' asked Lord Merrion. 'For the past twenty-four hours we have heard nothing but contradictions. One minute the country is in rebellion and Dublin is to be attacked. The next we hear everything is tranquil. Beresford is supposed to have said he wants action – a curfew and a search for arms in the city. Camden is almost cheerful, says there is no need for alarm – everything is under control.'

'Any news of Lord Edward?' asked Clarissa.

'They haven't removed the ball – his life is not considered in danger,' said Lady Abagail. 'One report says he is in great pain. Another that he is recovering so well that he'll soon be ready for the rope.'

'Should be nearly time for dinner.' Lord Merrion was consulting a great turnip of a watch.

'We'll get something, I'm not sure what,' said Lady

Abagail. 'Somehow no one had the heart to make preparations. Not knowing if you would arrive in Lucan or if you would come back again safely. We were so out of spirits last night, Ramage just brought us some cold meats. We went through hours of misery.'

Martha couldn't help wondering if it was the missing daughter or the missing dinner that gave the Merrions such hours of misery.

As Ramage appeared to announce dinner, Lady Abagail said, 'But, Andrew, we have never asked after your father. How inconsiderate of us. How is he? He was taken ill suddenly, was he not?'

'Very suddenly . . . we think it was the strain of the Kingston trial. Nothing would do him but to return home to Leixlip – you know how obstinate people can be at that age.'

'Indeed, I do.' A slight glance at Lord Merrion.

'But at home with his books and his claret he recovered remarkably. I'm only thankful he didn't insist on returning to Sligo. We had to tell him that as the castle is deserted at the moment, my brother being in England, it would be most uncomfortable. Not a bed aired. Not a cow killed for dinner.'

'Very refreshing to find children who discharge their duty to their parents – you will join us for dinner, won't you? We are just ourselves and George and Sophie.'

'I will never fail in my duty to you again, Mama,' promised Clarissa.

'George!' said Clarissa to Martha as they went down to the dining-room. 'I'm in for a real lecture.'

But George, who arrived just as they were seating themselves, had other matters on his mind. 'I take it,' he began, 'that you have heard the news?'

'What news?' Lady Abagail said fretfully. 'We haven't been anywhere or received anyone with all this worry.'

'Clarissa,' George seemed about to embark on the expected lecture when Lady Abagail urged, 'Never mind Clarissa. What is the news?'

'I had it from Bennett who had it from one of Camden's aides . . . so I think we may count on its veracity . . . you know that most of the news we are getting these days is plain rumour, but I flatter myself that I can tell the difference between . . .'

'Come to the point, George,' said Lady Abigail.

'The brothers Sheares were arrested this morning.'

Matilda who had just come into the room turned even paler – if that were possible. Martha looked at her questioningly. She gave an almost imperceptible shake of the head. So there was no news of James.

'Who are the Sheares brother?' asked Lord Merrion. 'Never heard of them in my life.'

'They're both barristers. John and Henry. Highly revolutionary ideas, I understand. They were part of the plot that Lord Edward was involved in.

'The word is that they made friends of a Captain Armstrong, a young militia officer. He was in a bookshop in Grafton Street and Henry Sheares deduced from his choice of books that he, too, was a revolutionary. They became friendly and Armstrong got hold of their plans. I would assume that Armstrong, quite properly, disclosed the plans, whatever they were, and the Government decided to arrest the brothers.'

'Plans? What plans?' But Lord Merrion's curiosity was diverted by the arrival of dinner. In spite of Lady Abigail's disclaimer, Ramage lifted up covers to display a roast chicken, a poached salmon and a stew of leveret as the centre attractions, fringed around with assorted dishes of peas, mushrooms and salads. Champagne appeared, as well as burgundy and claret.

'What Papa would describe as a little light supper,' said

Clarissa. 'I'm really hungry. Are you?'

Martha found that indeed she was. George was questioned further about the Sheares, but as he knew nothing more than he had told them and as the Merrions had never heard of them in the first place, the conversation drifted into other channels.

'Matilda has been such a help,' said Lady Abigail. 'I vow I don't know what I would have done without her. She took complete charge of Cecil and Cedric – that wretched James is still missing. Not a word from him. After all our kindness to him. And I thought him so reliable. Now it turns out he is a wild young man. Hallsworth told me, when I questioned him, that he wouldn't be at all surprised if he were in the United Irishmen. And that that was why he left – to prepare for this supposed rebellion.'

'Now that Lord Edward has been arrested, and these other fellows – whoever they are – I have no doubt but that this trouble will all blow over.' For once Lord Merrion was decidedly optimistic and drank a further few toasts to mark the occasion.

After dinner, while the Merrions and Dunboynes returned to the drawing-room, the four young people went to the morning-room.

'What did you tell Lady Abigail?' asked Martha as they assembled.

'That we wanted to plan costumes for a masked ball.'

'And she believed you?'

'Well why not? There is one planned at Mountjoy House next week.'

'Which may now never happen.' Andrew sounded sober. 'Lady Louisa told me yesterday of something her husband overheard a month or so ago. One cottier told another not to bother planting potatoes, that they'd never be dug.'

'The ring first,' said Clarissa. 'Let's ask Ramage.'

Rmage had been told about the theft by Breege. 'I made a few enquiries,' he said when he came in. 'Lanigan thinks he may be one of a gang of small criminals who sometimes band together to attack carriages coming home at night. But usually they're on their own. A friend of his has engaged to find out if one has a missing finger.

'On Saturday night, when news of the arrest of Lord Edward spread, the weavers from the Liberties and the butchers from Patrick Street surged into the streets around the castle, intent on rescuing Lord Edward. Every footpad and thief in the city joined in. Then there was a report that a squadron of cavalry was advancing and they all fled. The watchmen and soldiers picked up a number of people, especially those who were too drunk to get away.'

'And he *was* drunk.'

'So, Miss, he may well be in a prison somewhere.'

'Using the ring to barter his way out,' surmised Andrew. 'What prison would he be in?'

'They probably would have put him in the Royal Exchange, being near at hand. There's a cellar or two they throw drunks into. I'll get Lanigan to find out tomorrow.'

'I'll go with him. We can offer him a reward – if he still has the ring. And we'll check the pawn shops. Thanks, Ramage . . . and now I must be off, as soon as I take my leave of Lady Abigail. Trust me, Martha. I will do everything I can.'

When he was gone, Martha turned to Matilda.

'I didn't say anything to Andrew about James,' she said contritely.

Matilda gave a rather wan smile. 'It's probably just as well. I don't think he would be able to help. And it would be dangerous for him to get involved.'

'Have you any news?" asked Clarissa.

'I haven't had much opportunity to find out anything

since you left – I've been busy with Cedric and Cecil, not to mention Lady Abigail. I did manage to get a message to Miss Moore with Lanigan.'

'Matilda.' Clarissa went over and sat down beside her. 'You know a great deal more than you're telling us. I don't know whether we can help James or not. But you must tell us what you know.'

'I only know what Miss Moore told me. On the day of the Kingston trial there was a meeting. Lord Edward and Sam Neilsen wanted to get their supporters in the country to rise and march on Dublin. The Sheares brothers and Surgeon Lawless didn't want the attack on Dublin. They were convinced that the militia would join the cause and they wanted to wait. The two sides couldn't agree. The Sheares resigned and Lawless is fled, to France I believe. Now Lord Edward is in prison, the Sheares arrested. Only Sam Neilsen is left – and he's hopeless.

'James is somewhere out there waiting for the signal, probably not knowing what has happened or what is happening now.'

'Matilda, you can do nothing. Just hope and pray. James must have heard of the arrests. He'll know the plans are in disorder. He'll come back.'

As she prepared for bed, Martha thought about poor lonely James, a most unlikely revolutionary, waiting somewhere, in fear of his life, waiting for the call that now would never come.

13   A Search Party

At breakfast next morning, Lady Abigail ordered the carriage. She wanted to go shopping. Clarissa and Martha were to come with her, Matilda would stay behind with the twins. Lord Merrion's doubts about the wisdom of going into the city centre were swept aside. Ribbons had to be bought and ribbons would be bought.

But the shopping expedition was short-lived. As they approached the area around the Castle, they were stopped by soldiers. The whole area had been sealed off, they were told. Eight hundred yeomanry were searching the Liberties, house by house, street by street. Men and boys were being frogmarched into the Castle yard, their womenfolk running screaming behind them.

'This is intolerable!' Lady Abigail was furious. She hailed an armed soldier who was accompanying some of the prisoners. 'What's happening?'

'Orders from the Castle, Ma'am. We're searching for arms – we've already uncovered quantities. When we find any, the men are to be brought to the castle yard, to be flogged for more information. The houses are to be burned, furniture thrown out into the streets. We've just set fire to Rattigan's warehouse – he was one of Lord Edward's bodyguards.' He marched away.

Andrew came to Merrion Square later and they walked in the garden. They had traced the thief, a beggar by the

150

name of Carty, who had been thrown into the Royal Exchange jail. He had bartered the ring for his freedom. A prison guard now had it.

'Ironic,' finished Andrew. 'He would have been released this morning anyway. There are now so many prisoners that the goals are full. They have no room for common criminals. But, Martha, don't worry. We know where the prison guard lives. We'll get the ring back.

'We have a plan. Lanigan and William – you remember him from the ball – and I. We'll put it into operation tomorrow.'

'Andrew,' Martha hesitated for a moment. 'Can I ask you a question?'

'Of course!'

'Are you – were you – a United Irishman? You probably don't know but James, the tutor, is missing. Martha says he

was in the movement and that he could be arrested and tortured. She is very worried.'

'Poor James. But tell Matilda to keep her spirits up. The Castle thinks that the threat is past. I have no doubt but that he'll find his way home soon.'

'You haven't answered my question.'

'I'm glad we're in the garden. Out of earshot.' He smiled. 'I was at one stage. In the beginning many people joined because we wanted to make the ideals of the old Volunteers come true. We wanted to be a country, not a colony. To be able to manage our own affairs. To have equality for everyone. How did Wolfe Tone put it? "To unite the whole people of Ireland, to abolish the memory of past dissentions and to substitute the common name of Irishman in place of the denominations of Protestant, Catholic and Dissenter." But you know all this,' another smile, 'from your history books. How do they write about us? Hot-headed idealists? Impractical fools? Men with a vision?'

'You said you "were" a member. Why did you leave?'

'You've heard of Fitzwilliam,' Martha nodded. 'When he was made Viceroy we had high hopes. He was a liberal, he intended to change things. For a start he proposed to get rid of Beresford and Cooke, the core of the old diehard Castle set. They appealed to London. Fitzwilliam was recalled. His Viceroyalty lasted just two months!

'Some said that peaceful means could never achieve what we wanted. They wanted violence . . . I couldn't go along with it. I saw all the hideous suffering it could cause, the divisions in families. I could not face the thought that my brother in the militia or someone like Colonel Vesey would be sent to hunt me down. Or that I would have to take up arms against them. You remember Barrington's story that first night we met, about the pact he proposed to his cousin. We all laughed but it was a deadly jest.'

'I understand. Most people want peace.'

'Everyone does – in theory. But when people are driven too far, when their land is taken away, when they are denied almost all their rights, when they are tortured and imprisoned for wanting to live like human beings – something snaps.

'Tell me,' said Andrew, 'and it's the only thing about the future in which I'm interested. Did we achieve what we thought was impossible?'

Martha thought hard. All she could say was, 'Up to a point. Almost but not quite. But things are better . . .'

'Well, that wouldn't be too difficult!'

They had just reached the far end of the garden when a cry behind them made them turn. Matilda was running towards them.

'It's James, he's back. What are we to do?'

'Where is he?'

'In the kitchen. But he can't stay there. Hallsworth is luckily away but he'll return in an hour or two.'

'We'll have to tell Lady Abigail,' said Martha.

'She said she'd never have him back.'

'People say things like that, often without really meaning them. She'll take him back,' said Andrew confidently.

'There's something else,' Matilda burst out. 'He's wounded. On his way back some soldiers challenged him. He ran away and they fired. He was hit in the shoulder.'

'Where did this happen?'

'In a lane off Mount Street. The chased him but he was too fast.'

'With a bit of luck they won't know where he went,' said Andrew. 'So let's concentrate on Lady Abigail.'

They went into the house and while Andrew went down to the kitchen to see James, Martha and Matilda went up to the morning-room. Clarissa was already there with Lady Abigail. With relief Martha noted the absence of both Lord Merrion and George.

'Lady Abigail, we have something to tell you,' she began. 'I do hope it won't upset you.'

'Upset me? After Sunday, nothing could. What is it? You aren't planning to take another country trip?'

'James has come back.'

'Well, he can take himself right back to where he came from.'

'Lady Abigail, you can't turn him away. He's been in hiding in dreadful conditions for the past three days. He's wounded. He was almost captured on the way here.' Matilda burst into tears.

'Matilda, control yourself. What is it to you if that young rapscallion comes or goes?'

'They have an understanding,' said Clarissa. 'James and Matilda.'

'A romantic attachment? Under my own roof? This gets worse and worse . . . Where is he now?'

'In the kitchen.'

At that moment a loud hammering was heard at the door, and almost immediately Ramage appeared, three soldiers in red uniforms behind him.

'I'm sorry, your Ladyship. These persons just forced their way in.'

'Major Hayes at your service, Lady Abigail. My orders are to search the house for weapons, pikes and guns. Also for an injured man who was seen to run in this direction.'

'*This* direction? We are surrounded by houses. Do you intend to search every one?'

'We have our orders. We have received information on houses known to sympathise with Lord Edward.'

'And you come to us? All I can say is that your information is somewhat at fault. I know poor Lady Bellamount's house was searched, just because she is sister to Lord Edward . . . for which she got a handsome apology from the Duke of Portland. Nothing was found – as indeed you'll find nothing here. So go ahead and search and I'll have an apology from Lord Castlereagh.'

The major hesitated but did not withdraw.

For one sickening moment Martha thought Lady Abigail was going to abandon James to his fate, but she almost immediately addressed her,' Martha, before I forget, go down and see that that idle Jenny launders my shifts,'

Martha paused. Jenny? But Breege had said that Jenny had left. She looked at Lady Abigail who made a very slight nod of her head. 'And tell her to fold them neatly and put them in the housekeeper's press.'

As Martha flew from the room Lady Abigail's voice followed her. 'It's all to tiresome. All this upset. Servants can't come and go without risk of being apprehended. How we're managing I don't know . . . Ramage, show these gentlemen around. Take them to the attics. I believe that's where the pikes are usually stored. And make sure they don't disturb Cedric or Cecil.'

Martha couldn't help laughing as she rushed down the stairs to the kitchen. James, pale-faced and anxious looking, was sitting in a chair. Mrs Morris, the cook, had washed and bandaged his wound.

'Quick! We're going to dress him as a laundry-maid. Are there any clothes? We haven't time to go upstairs to get any. Lady Abigail mentioned the housekeeper's press.'

'Dress as a maid? They'd never be taken in by that.'

'You must. It's your only chance.'

In no time at all James was dressed in the dark-blue uniform and apron of a maid.

'Thank goodness, you're thin,' said Martha giving him a final check over. 'And with the tucked cap no one would ever know you're a man. You make a very likely looking maid!'

Shoes were a difficulty but Mrs Morris volunteered hers and led him into the laundry room with the injunction,

'Keep your hands under water. They're rather larger than usual.'

'We'd better go upstairs,' said Andrew. 'We have no business in the kitchen.'

In the drawing-room the tension was like a thin thread hanging in the air, a thread that could snap at any moment.

Aware of the soldier posted outside, Lady Abigail, Clarissa, Martha and Andrew talked away, about balls and dinners and assemblies and routs at such a rate that Martha felt he must be thinking what an idle spendthrift lot they were. Matilda said nothing, sitting with her hands so tightly folded that her knuckles were white.

After what seemed an interminable period, the Major came back.

'And what did you find?' asked Lady Abigail.

'Nothing, Lady Abigail. I regret the intrusion but I must remind you it is a duty we owe the public. We did receive information that Lord Edward had been here.'

'Well, *I* never set eyes on him. Isn't it a little late to be looking for him now – I understand he's in gaol?'

'The house was under suspicion, and the report of a man running in this direction meant we had to investigate.'

'Well, Major, I know you must do your duty. Let's hope we meet in more of a social atmosphere on another occasion. I'm only thankful that Lord Merrion wasn't here to learn that he is suspected of harbouring arms and revolutionaries. It would have been the death of him.'

When the soldiers had gone, there was an unearthly hush in the room. No one spoke. No one stirred. All eyes were on the door as if they expected the soldiers to burst in again.

Half an hour later, Lady Abigail rose and said briskly, 'Now I must go and see this stupid James.'

Matilda's face was one big smile. 'Lady Abigail, I can't ever thank you enough.'

'Then don't try. I'm at a loss to know why your generation don't trust their elders. Why didn't you tell me about James? He comes of a respectable family and if he gets this revolutionary nonsense out of his head you could do worse . . .as for you, Clarissa, and this secret you and Martha share, no doubt you'll tell me some day.'

As Clarissa and Martha gave each other a guilty stare, Lord Merrion limped into the room, wanting to hear all about the events of the afternoon, fulminating that he hadn't been there to give Major Hayes a piece of his mind, scathing about soldiers who didn't know a loyal citizen from a rebel, all the while looking forward to a good dinner which, in spite of all the upsets, he expected to be placed on the table shortly.

'How is James?' asked Martha when later that night Clarissa and Matilda came into her bedroom.

'Fine. It's only a surface wound. Fancy, in the shoulder, just like poor Lord Edward.'

'Where was he since Saturday?'

'He got a message that he should go to a house that had been agreed on beforehand to await instructions. Lord Edward was to leave Dublin that evening and James thought he would be one of the party escorting him. They met in Queen Street, in a public house. There they got word of Lord Edward's arrest. There was a plan to rescue him but I suspect most of them were so well on in drink that nothing was done.

'They dispersed and poor James has been hiding in one house or another ever since. The Sheares brothers were said to be in command but no instructions came from them. Then they were arrested yesterday. James' officer said there was going to be a huge search and told him to fend for himself.'

'Poor James!'

Matilda was weeping quietly to herself and Martha thought of the heartbreak of James and Matilda and all those who had risked their lives for the ideals of the United Irishmen. And would continue to do so through a terrible rebellion. All they wanted was a world of freedom and justice. And the only weapons they had were hope, a few stolen guns and pikes.

'Why didn't Lord Edward give up?' asked Martha. 'After the arrests at Bond's, after the split with the Sheares and Lawless, he must have known he was unlikely to succeed.'

'He was asked that. His answer was, "I am too deeply pledged to these men to be able to withdraw with honour." '

'He is a honourable man,' said Clarissa softly. 'He has the highest ideals. Whatever happens, history will be kind to him.'

'Have you heard of the green bough,' asked Matilda dream-
ily, as she intoned in a whisper.'

> What have you got in your hand?
> *A green bough.*
> Where did it first grow?
> *In America*
> Where did it bud?
> *In France.*
> Where are you going to plant it?
> *In the crown of Great Britain.*

When they had gone, Martha thought, 'To them, this is
the end, but it's only the beginning. Andrew was right. It's
just as well not to want to see into the future.'

She thought, too, about the ring. Tomorrow Andrew
would try again. She remembered the agony she had gone
through the night she had lost it and her panic about it ever
since. Yet tonight James could have been captured and be
now in Newgate under sentence of death. As Lord Edward
was, though no one knew it yet. Tomorrow the flame of
rebellion would be lit all over the country. Nothing could
quench it now. Death, destruction and suffering would soon
be the lot of countless thousands on either side. How trivial
her worries seemed. 'To drive away a sorrow,' she remembered her mother saying, 'suffer a greater one.'

But in spite of her attempts to come to terms with her situation she fell asleep wishing with all her heart that she was
were safely home again.

14 Waiting

Wednesday turned out to be the strangest day that Martha had ever spent, a day of comings and goings, of rumour and counter rumour, of certainty and uncertainty.

George had come in to reassure them. 'Everything is being done to make sure Dublin can't be taken. An extra regiment has been brought in. The artillery at Chapelizod is at full strength.'

'Useless,' growled Lord Merrion. 'The Castle can't be defended. There was a plan to surround it with barbed wire and supply hand grenades for the people inside . . .'

'Very comforting for us on the outside,' sniffed Lady Abigail.

'. . . but nothing came of it. The city is wide open. The canal bridges are not fortified. There is no means of blowing up those on the Liffey. The Royal Barracks would be easily stormed.'

'But they have fortified the Pigeon House,' said George.

'Near the quays. How convenient – if anyone should wish to make a quick crossing to England.' Lady Abigail sounded sarcastic.

The next visitor was Jonah Barrington. 'Called in just to let you know the latest. First we were ordered to report with the attornies' corps of yeomanry. Now all is countermanded. It seems all is well. Camden completely satisfied there is to be no general rising. The leaders have been arrested, the rank and file disarmed. I must say I'm glad

Captain Keogh and I won't have to put our pledges into operation . . . So, Miss Martha, you can go back to planning your costume for the ball at Mountjoy House . . .'

But later in the day, fresh rumours began to circulate from house to house, through a network of servants. Kildare and Meath were to rise that night . . . an attempt was to be made to rescue Lord Edward . . . all the counties around Dublin were to combine to attack the city . . . the country yeomanry had thrown in their lot with the rebels . . . the outgoing mail coaches were to be set on fire as a signal to the rest of the country . . . Lord Camden was to be assassinated.

At dinner, every rumour was chewed and digested as thoroughly as the sole and mutton.

But where was Andrew? He had promised to be back around three o'clock and now it was nearly seven. Martha escaped for a moment to the garden. She was in an agitated state when Matilda came out.

'He must have been arrested. Else why isn't he here. And no word. Oh, Matilda, I'm worried sick.'

Matilda said quietly, 'Do you think there will be a rising after all?'

'Yes, I'm afraid I do.' She didn't say why she was so sure.

'They say they're chalking the doors of homes where there are traitors. Would James be considered a traitor?'

'Surely not. He was told to go away.'

'We'd better go inside. I was sent out to fetch you.'

Lady Abigail's face was grim as she poured out tea. 'The latest news is far from reassuring. They say vast armies of rebels have assembled at Santry and Rathfarnham.'

'There's no cause for concern, m'dear.' After a good dinner, Lord Merrion, comfortably ensconced in his great wing armchair, brandy bottle conveniently at hand, was in euphoric mood. 'Probably just another rumour. Anyway, the soldiers will defend us.'

'You're probably right. With so many wild stories circulating, I can't think how anyone knows what is happening . . . In any event, let us do something useful instead of sitting around discomposing ourselves with idle gossip . . . Matilda, fetch the work-baskets.'

Matilda went away and returned with piles of white fabric and baskets of sewing implements, which a footman helped her to carry. Not Lanigan, Martha noted: he must not be back yet.

'We make shirts for the Reverend James Whitelaw of Saint Catherine's,' explained Clarissa. 'Matilda sews beautifully. My stiches are so scattered I wonder the shirts hold together at all.'

I'm sure mine will be just as bad,' said Martha.

The evening wore on as they sewed away in silence, each occupied with her own thoughts. Lord Merrion, half asleep, sat and nodded into space.

A footman came in to light the chandeliers and Lady Abigail called a halt to the work.

'Look!' said Clarissa who was at the window. 'The street lamp has gone out.'

'It's been put out,' said Lady Abigail. They went over to the windows and as they watched, one by one, the lights along the street and across the square went out, until the whole area was in shadowy gloom. 'The better for deeds of darkness,' said Lady Abigail.

A footman brought in a tray of hot chocolate which they drank in silence. Then Lady Abigail said, 'It's time we went to bed. We can do nothing more. Only wait and pray.'

Martha had determined not to go to bed. She must be up in case Andrew came back. She waited until Breege had gone downstairs, then dressed herself again and went down to the dining-room to wait.

The long, long night dragged by. Once she thought she heard a noise and started. But it was only the night watchman, in his long frieze cape and low crowned hat, with his crooked pole and lantern, calling out, 'Five o'clock. Past five o'clock and a fine morning.'

It was true. The night had passed. Dawn was breaking over the garden and bit by bit the trees, the shrubs, the stables, assumed their familiar shapes, changing from black and grey into the pale green of leaves, the pinks and lilacs of flowers, the dusty rose-red stone of the buildings.

There was a knock on the front door. A footman rushed to answer and there was Andrew, looking dishevelled and exhausted. But exultant!

'I have your ring!'

'It was all so simple in the end. It's hard to say why it took so long. As you know William and Lanigan were to help me, and our plan was to dress as yeomen and go to the house where the prison warden lodged, having marked it earlier – it is on Inns Quay.

'You probably heard all the talk that has been sweeping the city.' Martha nodded. 'We had arranged to borrow the uniforms from some men William knew. But first the yeomen were ordered to be on call. Then the order was cancelled. Then the order went out again. So no one would part with a uniform.'

'But how did you manage?'

'It was late last night. They had finally been told to assemble in Smithfield. Some of them went into a nearby tavern and it wasn't too difficult, as the night wore on, to persuade them to lend us a uniform or two. We couldn't get three so we sent William home and Lanigan and I went in search of the warden.

'We were lucky. We only had to show ourselves in our uniforms and he fell to his knees in terror and produced the ring. I think he thought we were going to kill him . . .

'We went back to Smithfield where everything was in turmoil. No one knew what was happening. Or who was in command. Or what they were supposed to be doing. It took us the rest of the night to return the uniforms and make our way back here. We had to be so careful. Militia and yeoman were all over the place, in the mood to fire at anything that moved . . .

'To sum up. Here I am and there is your ring!'

He placed it on the middle finger of her right hand and as she looked at it the sun lit up the red fire in its inner depths.

'Oh, Andrew, I can never thank you enough.'

'It was little enough. Though I wonder at myself. Going to all that trouble so that you can leave me . . . Come, let us have a last walk in the garden.'

Arm in arm they strolled down the gravel path to the lilac

bushes and the nostalgic fragrance stole over them.

'I don't want to go back, Andrew.'

'And I don't want you to go back either. I wish with all my heart you could stay. But I must think of *you*. You know how uncertain are the times ahead. Suppose something happened to me? What would your position be? With no family, you would be totally dependent on others . . . So there really is no choice. You belong in your own time – you must go back to your home and your family.

'Just think of us sometimes. Think of us as more than usurpers who came in and took over the land, dispossessing those who were here before. Many of us do care. We hate the injustices, the inequality, the poverty . . .

'The Beresfords, the Clares and Castlereaghs are only one side of the coin. When you think of them think also of those who tried, and are still trying, to change things. Of Lord Edward, Wolfe Tone, Grattan and Charlemont, the Duke of Leinster, John Philpot Curran . . . did you know that he writes poetry? Not at all bad! There is one which seems particularly apposite to us at this very moment. Let me see if I can remember it:

> *If sadly thinking, and spirits sinking,*
> *Could more than drinking our griefs compose –*
> *A cure for sorrow from care I'd borrow*
> *And hope tomorrow might end my woes.*
>
> *But since in wailing there's naught availing,*
> *For Death, unfailing, will strike the blow;*
> *Then, for that reason, and for the season,*
> *Let us be merry before we go!*
>
> *A wayworn ranger, to joy a stranger,*
> *Through every danger my course I've run.*
> *Now, death befriending, his last aid lending,*
> *My griefs are ending, my woes are done.*

No more a rover, or hapless lover,
Those cares are over, my cup runs low;
Then, for that reason, and for the season,
Let us be merry before we go.'

His voice died away and there was stillness for a while. Then resuming his old bantering tone he said, 'The servants will soon be astir. Breege will be looking for you.'

'What will you tell them?'

'Don't worry. Clarissa and I will think of something.'

'She's very resourceful.'

'So I've discovered.'

'I'm sorry I can't see her before I go. Can you tell her how much I enjoyed everything – well almost everything! She was so kind to me. Give her my fondest farewell. And Lady Abigail too, and Breege. Also say good-bye for me to Matilda and James – I hope everything works out for them.

'And, oh, I nearly forgot. Make sure the Merrions don't go to Wexford.'

'You can count on me.' He picked a sprig of lilac and gave it to her saying, 'Now make your wish.' His lips brushed hers lightly.

She turned the ring twice and wished – to be home again.

Her eyes began to feel heavy and when they closed she could not open them again. The same strange feeling of giddiness came over her. Then everything went blank . . .

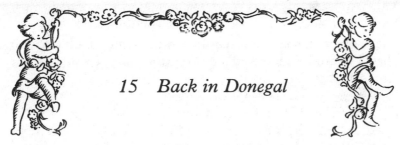

15 Back in Donegal

'What a thrilling story!' said Lucy when Gran had finished.
'I wish I'd thought of going back to such an exciting time.
Mine wasn't half as dramatic.'

'But I didn't wish for that part of it. It came with the
ball.'

'Gran, were you frightened?'

'Very. I'd forgotten just how much until I relived it again.
That evening when nobody knew what was happening,
when the lights started going out – I was really afraid.'

'But you knew that nothing could happen to you?'

'At the back of my mind, I suppose I did. Yet in some
strange way I didn't. It was like having a bad dream, being
really terrified, and yet being unable to realise that it *is* only
a dream. It was something like that.'

'I've lots of questions. But tell me first: what happened
when you got back?'

'Mother and Father were in my bedroom. They told me
I'd slept for twenty-four hours and they couldn't wake me.
Mother, in particular, was really afraid I'd never wake up
again! I could see that she had been crying. Father just took
my hand and held it for ages. But from then on things were
different. They let me go back to Frau Hassler for music
lessons, and all the endless washing and ironing of shirts
and the darning of socks stopped – Mother got someone in
to give her a hand.

'You see, until that birthday, I don't think they realised

how constricted my life was. They would have thought they had given me everything. A comfortable home, plenty to eat, clothes – what more could I want? They didn't realise that I wanted freedom. To learn about life. To be sixteen, not forty-six!'

'When did you meet Grandfather?'

'A year later. At another dance in the school house. We liked each other, did what we called a "line" in those days and got married when I was twenty-one.'

'Gran, you don't have to answer this question if you don't want to. How did you like him – compared with Andrew?'

'That's a very hard question. Andrew was my first love and your first love is always special. I never really got over him. But I respected and admired John. He was a fine man. Very easy and tolerant. We got on well together. Then the children came along and my life was so taken up with them and the farm that I hardly had time to think.'

'The lilac? Was Mrs. Shovlin right in thinking there was some mystery about a lilac-bush?'

'Yes, indeed! When John brought me home after our wedding to the farmhouse that the Shovlins now have – that was our first home – the lilac was in bloom. It was a magnificent tree, so fragrant, laden with blossom. I picked a sprig – and burst into tears. Everything came flooding back. The dinner, the ball, Andrew, the first walk in the garden and the last. I was inconsolable. Poor John rightly thought there was a romantic connection, but being the man he was he never asked me about it. The following day when I was out, he got an axe and chopped it down, to save me the heartache of reliving whatever memory had reduced me to tears. I was sorrier about that than anything . . . and now you tell me it's in bloom again. I'm so glad.'

'What happened to Andrew?'

'Andrew? History rarely records the lesser people. Remember Shakespeare:

When beggars die there are no comets seen,
The Heavens themselves blaze forth the death of princes.

I looked up most of the people I had met – I'll tell you about them another time. But back to Andrew . . . I had a strange experience several years after I was married.

'It was over near Sligo – John was buying some stock from a local farmer. There was a graveyard nearby and I walked about looking at the tombstones. It was overgrown with ivy and I could hardly make out the lettering. It was, "To the memory of . . ." '

'Yes,' prompted Lucy.

' "Andrew Morrison, Earl of Rossinver.'

'But his brother was the earl.'

'He must have died. Maybe been killed in the Rebellion, like Lord Mountjoy and so many others.'

'When did Andrew die?'

'I couldn't decipher that, as part of the stone was chipped away. But I could make out, "And of his wife, Cla . . ." The end of that word had gone too.'

'Clarissa!'

'Who knows? This is all just supposition. But I'd like to think he did get back to his beloved estate in the country instead of having to live in the city. The Rossinvers seem to have died out. I tried to look them up in some local guide-books but I never did find out much.'

'Gran, did you like these people? They all got their lands in the plantations, didn't they? They weren't really Irish, were they?'

'That's a very large question, Lucy. How far back do you go to get a true native Irishman, one who never came in on the wings of an invasion?

'The one thing I did learn from those seven days was not to see life as black and white. There were some savage Irish chieftains and some very caring landlords like the Leinsters.

'Years later I came across a piece of Synge in which he is remembering the garden at Glanmore Castle which belonged to his uncle: "In this garden one seemed to feel the tragedy of the landlord class, and of the innumerable old families that are quickly dwindling away. These owners of the land are not much pitied at the present day or much deserving of pity; and yet one cannot quite forget that they are the descendants of what was at one time, in the eighteenth century, a high-spirited and highly cultivated aristocracy."

'That was how they appeared to me. Not the Beresfords, the Clares and the Castlereaghs. But Andrew, Clarissa and her family, Jonah Barrington, William, Colclough . . . they were such fun. I know they had a lot of money and an easy way of life, but there was a gaiety about them that I particularly admired.'

'Gran, tell me, what was the very best memory of all.'

'Apart from Andrew? Oh, the ball! I'll never be able to describe to you how wonderful it was. The music, the dancing, the clothes, the people, the elegance of the ballroom, the chandeliers, the conversations . . .'

'And the worst memory?'

'Undoubtedly the night I lost the ruby ring. Not that there weren't other bad moments! The saddest was of the time that James came back, seeing Matilda and him weeping over Lord Edward and the collapse, as they thought, of the Rebellion. Good memories, bad memories . . . always remember roses have their thorns . . . Now, I want to show you something.' She took a green velvet pouch from her handbag and said, 'Open it.'

Lucy did and drew out a large shell.

'The gloves, the Limerick gloves! You brought them home.' Gently Martha took out the gossamer fine gloves, now a faded yellow and frayed around the seams.

Lucy gazed at them until at last she said in an awed voice,

'Better put them away, Gran, or they might fall apart altogether.'

Martha folded the gloves again and carefully replaced them, first in the walnut shell and then in the velvet pouch. 'I also took home the sprig of lilac. I pressed it and I'll show it to you some some day. Sentimental some people might say, I suppose!'

'Haven't you finished talking yet?' Paul McLaughlin came into the bedroom. 'I never knew such a pair. Natter, natter, natter. For hours at a time . . . Gran, I think you should have your nap. Lucy, would you feel like giving your mother a hand with the supper? Robert is setting the table, complaining that he seems to be the only kitchen hand around these days.'

'Sure,' Lucy slid off her chair. 'Let's hope he doesn't break everything.'

When she went up to call Gran later, she was still asleep. On the pillow, her face looked young, unlined and carefree, the face of the girl with whom Andrew had fallen in love in the strange twilight world of 1798.

Epilogue

The Rebellion of 1798 was a failure. It was suppressed savagely; the leaders were either executed or fled, some to France, some to America. The rank and file of the rebels were forced into the British army and navy, or transported to Australia – there is a war memorial in Sydney to the men of '98. One group ended their days in the army of the King of Prussia. Nothing changed for the vast body of peasants, but emigration was soon averaging 50,000 a year.

The direct result of the Rebellion was the Union of Ireland with Britain. It was approved in the Irish House of Commons by 65 votes, in the House of Lords by 69 votes. Thus, with the help of bribery on a massive scale – fifteen new baronies, fifteen promotions in the peerage and promises of jobs – the Irish Parliament voted itself out of existence. The Catholic hierarchy, with the promise of Catholic emancipation, were solidly behind the Union: the Orange party opposed it, probably for the same reason.

The Act of Union passed into law on 1 January 1801. The Union did not bring the peace and prosperity that the English Prime Minister, William Pitt, had hoped for.

The principal characters

Lord Clonmell, the Chief Justice, died on the day the Rebellion broke out. Lord Clare lived to see the Union, died a year and a month later. Lord Castlereagh became British Foreign Secretary, and Edward Cooke, one of the most important of the Castle officials, served with him; he committed suicide in 1822. Byron mentioned him: *I met death along the way, He had a mask like Castlereagh.*

The Beresfords, who had opposed the Union, prospered; one of them became Primate of Ireland.

Lord Edward lingered until the beginning of June. Camden refused to allow any of the family to visit him but Lord Clare, surprisingly, defied the ban and actually accompanied Louisa Conolly and Henry Fitzgerald to Newgate Prison where they saw the dying Lord Edward. His brother, the Duke of Leinster, suffered for his public support of the United Irishmen. His affairs, which were in a bad state, were almost totally ruined by the Rebellion., And that same fatal June, his wife Aemilia died.

Lady Edward proved to be somewhat of a problem. She was expelled by the Irish government, and because Lord Edward had been branded as a traitor the estate he left her was confiscated. The English government didn't want her in England either, so, leaving her three children to be brought up by Emily, the Dowager Duchess of Leinster, she went to Hamburg where she lived on an allowance of £200 a year. She married the United States Consul there, Mr Pitcairn. She never saw her son again.

The Sheares brothers were executed, and Oliver Bond died in prison. Samuel Neilson went to America, where he died in 1803. Surgeon Lawless rose to the rank of major-general in the French army. Arthur O'Connor, one of the dominant figures in the Directory of the United Irishmen, the man Lucy Fitzgerald wanted to marry, was put on trial in England and acquitted – on the morning that Lord Edward died. After an investigation in Ireland, he went to France, married a French aristocrat and acquired a chateau in Lorraine. He died in his bed in 1852 at the age of eighty-nine.

The French made another attempt at invasion, in September 1798. Wolfe Tone, who was with them, was arrested at Buncrana and found guilty of high treason: whereupon he cut his throat. Ironically, Tone the patriot and Reynolds the informer were married to sisters.

After Robert Emmet's unsuccessful rising in 1803, Sarah

Curran, his beloved, was harshly treated by her father; she married a surgeon and was dead within five years. Curran himself drifted into obscurity, took a Government job after the Union and died in London in 1817, 'melancholy and embittered'.

Henry Grattan, dressed in the uniform of the old Volunteers, made an impassioned speech against the Union on 26 May, 1800. He continued to fight for Catholic Emancipation but his petitions and bills were rejected in 1813, 1817 and 1819 (coincidentally, all in the month of May). He died in 1820 and the British Government had him buried in Westminster Abbey.

Jonah Barrington had ambitions to be made Solicitor-General, rather optimistically as he had opposed the Union, but Clare and Castlereagh blocked him. He was made a judge and a baronet but because he misappropriated funds paid into his court he was removed from the Bench – though it is suggested that the real reason for this may have been because he was resuming publication of his *Historic Memoirs,* exposing the corruption and bribery leading to the Union. He died in Versailles in 1824.

His cousin, Captain Keogh, was hanged and Barrington saw his head on a spike outside Wexford courthouse.

The informers

The Castle had a chain of informers. Thomas Reynolds, the kinsman of Lord Edward, the man whose house was plundered by the army, was one. So was Francis Magan, a young Catholic barrister, who was made a member of the National Directory of the United Irishmen. Probably the most important was Leonard McNally. As a barrister, working on the defence of United Irishmen, he was in an unique position to brief the Castle on plans and personalities. No one quite knows why he became an informer.

Author's Note

I would like to thank Maureen McIntyre of Glenties Library for all the help she has given me; also Paul Gallagher and Mrs Campbell of Letterkenny Library.

The books I consulted in writing *Martha and the Ruby Ring* were:

Barrington, Jonah. *Personal Sketches.*
Craig, Maurice. *Dublin 1660–1880.*
Dickson, Charles. *The Wexford Rising in 1798.*
Dunlevy, Mairead. *Dress in Ireland.*
Fitzgerald, Brian. *Emily, Duchess of Leinster.*
Fitzpatrick, W.J. *The Sham Squire.*
Gerard, Frances. *Picturesque Dublin, Old and New.*
Guinness, Desmond, and Ryan, William. *Irish Houses and Castles.*
Lecky, W.E.H. *A History of Ireland in the Eighteenth Century,* Vol. IV.
Lindsey, John, *The Shining Life and Death of Lord Edward Fitzgerald.*
Maxwell, Constantia. *Country and Town in Ireland under the Georges; Dublin under the Georges.*
O'Reilly, Sean, and Rowan, Alistair. *Lucan House.*
Pakenham, Thomas. *The Year of Liberty.*
Somerville Large, Peter. *The Triumph of Elegance.*

Yvonne MacGrory
November 1993

YVONNE MacGRORY is Donegal born and bred. Her maiden name was McDyer, and she is a niece of Father James McDyer of Glencolumbkille.

She trained as a SRN, and now lives in Kilraine, near Glenties, County Donegal, with her husband Eamon and three children – Jane, Donna and Mark.

Her interests are reading, particularly local history, and she also sketches and gardens. She likes participating on quiz teams and doing crosswords.

Her first book was *The Secret of the Ruby Ring,* which won the Bisto Award for the best first novel of 1991. It has been reprinted several times, and published in the United States by Milkweed Editions.

TERRY MYLER trained at the National College of Art in Dublin, and also studied under her father, Séan O'Sullivan, RHA. She specialises in illustration and has done a lot of work for The Children's Press. Titles include *The Secret of the Ruby Ring, The Silent Sea, The Children of the Forge,* the Tom McCaughren 'Legend' books, *Save the Unicorns, Fionuala the Glendalough Goat, Henry & Sam & Mr Fielding: Special Agents, The Witch at Batsford Castle, The Witch who Couldn't,* and the Cornelius Rabbit books.

She lives in the Wicklow hills, with her husband, two dogs and a cat. She has one daughter.